Refuge for the Damned

By Vanessa Haney

Acknowledgements

As always, thank you to my early draft readers: Sheri, Blanca, Kelly and Amanda. You love these characters as much as I do and believe me, they love you back. Your careful scrutiny and thoughtful input helps me bring them to life.

I never include Mike in the early draft reader thanks because he witnesses it all, from the blank page to publishing day. That includes long weekends spent in ghost towns, many miles of hiking in the mountains, piles of research all over the kitchen, and enough anxious author energy to power the house. I've never once heard him complain about any of it. Except hiking. He complains incessantly while hiking. But unless I'm about to wander off a ledge, he is quiet on the trails when he knows I'm onto an idea. For all of this, there are no words.

To hear your twenty-two-year-old say, "I'm proud of you, Mom," is the coolest thing ever, and I get to hear it all the time. Thank you, Connor.

Also by Vanessa Haney

Heaven's Watch Series
Heaven's Lost (book 1)
Heaven's Watch (book 2)
Heaven's Call (book 3)
The Devil's Memories (book 4)

The Damned Series
Refuge for the Damned (book 1)

Short Stories
The Chuparosa Chronicle – Volume One

Author's Confessions

This book is a western, a supernatural western, but still a western. For the most part, I tried to maintain historical accuracy but, in some instances, the facts do not line up with the story. For example, The Bradshaw Mountain Railroad from Prescott to Phoenix was not in service until 1901, but our main characters rode that train in 1885; the Planetary Pencil Pointer was not patented until 1896; and, in 1885, the area that would be established as McGuireville in 1910 would have been known as Beaver Creek.

Chapter One

"You said dead or alive," Jess Carson reminded the Marshal.

He dismounted in front of the undertaker's shop and gestured to the man unceremoniously draped across the horse next to him.

"That I did." Marshal Derrick "Dusty" Dorman lifted the man's head to get a better look at his face and then waved a hand in front of his nose against the smell of the two-day old corpse.

Dusty handed the reins to the undertaker who was standing by. "I suppose Bill Taylor can start all the fires he wants to now that he's rotting in Hell."

Bill Taylor had liked to watch things burn. Trees, churches, people, they all gave him the same thrill. Jess caught up with him, whiskey bottle in one hand, torch in the other, after he'd set fire to the dry brush around a homestead on the outskirts of Clarkdale, Arizona. The flames moved quickly toward the house and Jess would have had to warn the family, letting Taylor get away, if not for the young boy who'd been spying on them from behind the stable. The kid ran shouting to those inside, not about the encroaching fire, but about the gunman who was, "about to kill a dirty criminal—right in front of the house!" At the time, Jess wasn't completely sure about that, but at least the family would be safe and he could focus on taking Taylor down, one way or another.

It would have been easier if Adam had been there. Jess was reasonably sure that as Bill lumbered toward him swinging the fiery torch, Adam would have agreed with his decision to shoot the arsonist. But even after being on his own for so long, Jess still caught himself looking to his left for confirmation. There was no time for second guessing though. The family would need help to save their home, and Bill Taylor was not going to come along quietly.

Bill's torch caught the arm of Jess's coat during the fight, but he was able to get off a poorly aimed shot before hitting the dirt to roll out the fire. Thick smoke billowed around them as Jess stood frowning over Bill's writhing body. Bleeding out through the belly was a bad way to die but Bill Taylor was a bad man and, for what Bill probably thought was too long a minute, Jess even considered letting him burn to death. But Jess wasn't a fan of poetic ends, and there would have been no payout for an unidentifiable corpse.

Jess followed Dusty to the jail, stopping short as he stepped over the threshold. Though he stood right next to the faded 'Wanted' poster, the likeness of he and Adam Colter was so bad that the Marshal hadn't put it together. Not yet.

Nearly two years had passed since Betty robbed that bank in Flagstaff, getting Jess shot in the process. He rubbed absently at the place where the bullet had torn through his chest. And it had only been a year since he'd left the Hinojosa ranch in search of Adam. They did not share blood, but in Jess's mind, Adam was his big brother and his only family.

The bank cashier's bullet somehow missed his heart but had damaged his left lung. Clemente Hinojosa's family took excellent care of Jess, in fact, he suspected that the elder Mrs. Hinojosa had literally worked magic over his wounds. He would never again be able to run uphill without gasping for air, but that wasn't a favorite activity of his anyway.

When he wasn't hunting criminals for pay, the only activity that interested Jess was searching for Adam. Betty had let them take the fall for the robbery and the Hinojosas weren't able to hide both men from the law. Adam left him in their care and headed for Cottonwood, but he was long gone by the time Jess was well enough to follow. His trail had gone cold outside of Clarkdale, but Jess was determined to search every sweeping mile in Arizona until he found him.

Dusty rummaged around in the unfamiliar rolltop desk until he found the ledger. The Marshal had requested that Bill Taylor's body be brought to McGuireville where he was doing double duty. McGuireville had been without a sheriff since the last one was shot to death over the wife of a miner.

Dusty spoke out loud as he wrote, "James Carter…"

Jess had been working under the alias of James Carter for some months and he grimaced every time he heard it out loud. It didn't help his quest any that Adam was likely traveling under an assumed name as well.

"…paid two hundred dollars for the capture of Bill

Taylor–Escaped Arsonist," Dusty continued, "and let's see...today is the twelfth of March, eighteen hundred and eighty-five." He counted out some bills from a cash box and handed the stack to Jess, asking, "Where're you headed next?"

"Not sure," Jess lied.

"You're pretty good at this, but bounty hunters don't have the best reputations." Dusty stared at him thoughtfully, "Ever thought about legitimate law enforcement?"

Not good enough to find Adam, Jess thought to himself, but mumbled, "My reputation wasn't likely to suffer much."

Though they'd served as deputies more than once, Adam had a particular distaste for the law.

"That little tin star makes an awfully big target," he'd said.

"Well, if you change your mind," Dusty offered, "there are worse places than McGuireville to settle down."

"And I've been to most of them," Jess chuckled.

Checking off the completed job in his book, he noted the pay and divided the amount in half, saving back half of everything he made, just in case he found Adam in a bad way.

Dusty stood and slapped him on the shoulder. "Even though you're the one who's flush, I'll buy you a drink."

Jess would rather have not. He was expecting a message at Fort Verde that would hopefully dictate his next destination and that poster, bad likeness or not, made him nervous. Still, he didn't want to cause offense and left with Dusty for The Well.

As the two men pushed through the swinging doors, the dark figure of Mark Chisolm, his face hidden as always by the wide brim of his hat, slipped into the jail. He tore down the 'Wanted' poster and crossed his feet on top of the desk, waiting for Marshal Dorman to return.

Jess's stomach rumbled as he thought to himself that what The Well passed off as whiskey should have been considered a crime. After making a note about the quality—or lack thereof—he reached overhead, his long body cracking and popping as he stretched.

Jess had started what he called *keeping track* in a little notebook while recovering at the Hinojosa ranch. It began as a list of funny things he didn't want to forget to tell Adam once they were reunited and soon became a record of clues as to Adam's whereabouts. Then, in his loneliness, it had turned into a travel journal of sorts. He recorded details about the criminals he tracked but also the nicest lakes and the greatest rivers for fishing, as well as the best restaurants and the worst hotels.

He put his pencil away and opened and closed his fist a few times to loosen up the achy muscles in his wrist. *Jesus,* he thought, *you're turning into a broken-down old man.* But at thirty-six, his body had survived all sorts of assaults that might have killed someone else, and he had Adam to thank for that.

When Jess was just fifteen years old, his right arm had been crushed in the grip of a madman. The murderous Walter Sallow kicked in the door of the little house young Jess shared with his grandfather and straight away bit into the old man's neck. Jess tried to fight him, but Walter was too fast and too strong for the boy, stronger than anyone Jess had ever known. Walter grabbed him by the arm and threw him across the room where he drifted in and out of consciousness, watching in horror as Walter appeared to drink his grandfather's blood.

Hunting Walter for a similar crime, Adam Colter rode up to their house the next day like a gift from God, or whichever deity oversaw such dark events. At the time, Jess was afraid Adam would think he was crazy if he mentioned that he thought he saw Walter drinking his grandfather's blood. It was an unnatural thing to do, even for a monstrous man like that. Jess told himself it was probably a trick of his mind anyway and kept that detail to himself. It was the only thing he'd never shared with Adam.

In the end it didn't matter because Adam killed Walter, nursed Jess as he recovered from the infection in his shattered arm, and patiently worked with him, making sure he was more competent as a lefty than he ever was with his right hand.

From those first days together, the two became a devoted brotherhood, separated only because Betty framed them for murder. Adam had always been a— more or less—God-fearing man, but Jess would claim to have no religion except that he was certain Walter Sallow, Betty Brown, Bill Taylor and all of their ilk were born of the Devil himself; and he did not care what hunting down those demons did to his reputation.

He spread out some oats for Pepper, his dark dapple-gray mare, who dipped her head for a long cool drink while he dropped a line in the Verde River. Just outside of dry and gritty McGuireville, the river valley was lush with sycamore trees, and well-known for its abundance of fish. Jess wanted nothing more than to relax on the bank with a fat flakey dinner after the harrowing days he'd spent on Taylor's trail.

He stiffened after a scan of his surroundings revealed two Indians about three hundred yards away. The Apache wars in that area had been raging for years, but Jess was not a soldier and, if pressed, he wouldn't be able to say that he supported their mission. Still, the folks upriver would never assume he meant them no harm.

The Indians were a man on horseback keeping watch over a young woman as she crouched on the bank collecting water. The man noticed him and shifted defensively on his horse, but did not raise the rifle from his lap. Jess's pulse quickened. It seemed as though those particular Apaches had no interest in a fight with him, but he could not allow himself to be confident about that.

He tried to make sure that his movements would be interpreted not as harmless but at least nonaggressive and cautiously went about his business. The fishing pole bobbed, and he turned the bulk of his attention to hauling up a razorback sucker so big that it nearly broke his line. When he looked back, the man on the horse gave him an approving nod and then the girl stood, strung her water bladders together and hung them across the back of the horse. Her guardian offered his hand, and she effortlessly swung her body astride. When the girl's arms were secured around his waist, he nodded to Jess once more, and they rode off.

Jess returned the gesture and let his breath out hard and only after they disappeared into the woods did he deal with the razorback on the line. It thrashed so violently that he snagged a finger when pulling the hook from its mouth. He swore and smacked the fish on a rock, then backed the hook out of his skin, grimacing at the small chunk of flesh he lost during the process. Dazed but not unconscious, the fish began flopping again and Jess dropped the hook in the grass, barely getting his knife into his dinner's belly before it jumped back in the river.

Without dropping his guard, he made a fire and especially enjoyed that belligerent fish. Laying back on the grass, he watched Pepper finish her oats and then took note of the now familiar stitch in his chest that came with each breath of cool air. There was no point in courting pneumonia. It would be a cold night and, bad whiskey or no, he was grateful to Marshal Dorman for delaying his departure so he could spend it in a nice warm room back in town.

It might have just been his close encounter with the Apache pair, but Jess could not shake an eerie sensation that settled over him as he packed up to go. The sunset streamed through the trees, creating wide planks of light through which he caught a glimpse of something lurking above that glowed with a turquoise hue. It was gone in the blink of an eye, but still his heartbeat sped up again. Certain that it wasn't just a reflection of the light; he searched the area but found nothing except more uneasy feelings.

Perhaps the Indians had seen it too—or felt it. It would be nice to talk to them about it as he was sure they shared a mutual respect for the oddities in the woods, but even if they were friendly, they were long gone. Pepper gave him a nudge with her head as if she was uncomfortable too, seeming as happy as Jess was when they finally headed back the way they came.

The long-limbed man-shaped thing hiding in the trees tucked his shiny necklace into his shirt and let the Indians pass. The warriors and their children were a delicacy, but typically under spiritual protection and difficult to procure. With so many new human breeds arriving daily to the west, the Indigenous ones had been relegated to little more than emergency sustenance.

He shimmied down and ran his fingers along the grass until he found the hook, holding it up to what remained of the daylight. The metal was dark red with a sticky coating of Jess's blood, and closer inspection revealed the small bit of skin had been left behind as well.

He'd first noticed the bounty hunter as Jess Carson tracked down the one who lit fires. The human sport of stalking one another still confused him, even after living among them for decades. While he found it distasteful in general to hunt one's own kind, quite often females were the targets of their violence. He questioned the wisdom of committing such acts against the only ones who could perpetuate the species but, overall, considered the act of preying on the weak and the small to be the most unforgivably shameful aspect of humanity.

The bounty hunter's awkward movements compensated for old injuries, but Jess was neither weak nor small. The disabilities had made him strong, unpredictable, and dangerous—vastly underestimated by the now dead fire starter.

The man-shaped thing had followed Jess to the

bank of the river, captivated by the aura of loss that hovered around him and breathing in the musty scent of loneliness mingled with rage. He could feel Jess's fear of a confrontation with the Indians but also his resolve if the situation had come to that. He could almost taste his bravery in the face of such vulnerability. Almost, but not yet; that was to be savored later.

He'd learned that the bounty hunter took every opportunity to fish, and until that day it was the only time he ever truly relaxed. The rippling of the water had a hypnotic effect on him that the man-shaped thing found impossible to recreate for himself. Carefully packing the hook, he practically vibrated with excitement. Such a man would be a deliciously fierce adversary, and so it was decided right then that Jess Carson was the one, and it would be a most gratifying hunt.

Chapter Two

The cave where he lived was situated far back in the wall of a narrow canyon over a mostly dry gulch. Though the creek had been dammed up north, a dribble of snow runoff kept a shallow reservoir full in the spring and afternoon monsoon rainstorms provided water in the summer, most of the time.

The man-shaped thing stopped to fill a bucket before heading up a rickety homemade ladder. It was a tedious chore but, in his enthusiasm, it would not do to make a costly mistake.

First focusing on the most important spell of the night, he unwrapped Jess's fishhook from a linen handkerchief, careful not to have wiped off any of the blood. Using a piece of twine soaked in boiled blackberry brambles, he secured the hook to a candle carved with symbols few had ever seen and hung it to burn upside down while he worked out the rest of his plan.

It would have been better if the bones he'd gathered were torn from a kill of his own and dried over a few months, with the fresh rot permeating his quarters with fumes of success. But the bounty hunter was always on the move and there was no time. The burlap sack he emptied on the floor of the cave contained several tiny bones gathered from the cemetery plots of a family with, based on so many little crosses, no talent for raising children.

His current abode had nothing like the crystal coated, opulent walls he'd taken for granted on the Other Side, but it was near a semi-reliable water source and situated in such a way that a fire could not be seen by any passersby.

Fire. A necessary element, but it conjured too many memories of his last day at home and was always extinguished as soon as possible. The last day, when he was betrayed by his own family. Set aflame along with his most precious tools and spells, chasing clouds through the desert until, just in time, the rainstorm saved his life. *Saved.* If that's how one described smoldering and exposed, nearly skinless, ugly and alone.

He piled the bones in a stone mortar and squatted as close as he dared in front of what had dwindled to little more than embers. Mesmerized by the grinding of the pestle, he allowed himself to become flooded with memories of the old days. Foley, he was once called. Before being given the label, among others, the Thing That Eats Hearts. At that time, he'd only eaten one—a detail that his mother assigned little importance.

Once revered on the Other Side for his power, his charm, and his thick masculine build, Foley was now cursed and reviled, stripped of his titles and banished to the human Side. Accused of savagery and forbidden alchemy, he often laughed to himself as, before being sent away, he could never have imagined the astounding cruelty that the humans were capable of. He'd learned a lot from them since then.

As the little bones turned to dust, he added a desiccated scorpion tail and a handful of saguaro spikes, working the concoction into a soft powder which he then poured into a small leather pouch. From a trunk in the back of the cave, Foley selected a fine shirt and vest to wear with pinstriped trousers into which he pocketed the dangerous potion.

When the candle burned down, Foley threaded the fishhook with a short piece of twine and whispered a few words while securing it to his prized necklace. He checked the mirror, making sure the beads—turquoise and juniper strung on a thin rope of moistened mesquite bark—were displayed over the vest before topping the ensemble with a silk jacket and a short-brimmed black hat. The hat was tasteful and hid the fact that his once flowing blonde hair now hung in a few long greasy strands that he refused to cut, on principle.

That part of the country was uncultured at best, but if he was to be seen, Foley preferred to affect a more cosmopolitan image. The juxtaposition of his elegant clothing and his unsettling form was often enough to clear a room, allowing him free access to costly necessities. In this case Foley intended to make a commanding impression on Jess Carson, lest there be any confusion about the game that was about to be played.

Foley's mirror hung askew on a wooden pike hammered into the wall of his cave. The mirror was oval shaped, seated in a thin but ornate brass frame and large enough that he could gaze at his entire head up close, but small enough to travel with.

Even stricken with such a ghastly form, Foley's vanity was unmatched if only because he was certain that someday he would create a spell strong enough to reverse what had been done to him—a spell that would negate the necessity of the beads. Though Carson's blood was likely to extend his life a good long time, he would prefer to be rid of the curse entirely. He often stared in the mirror for hours, no longer dejected by his image, but determined to change it.

Foley slid the mirror into a velvet drawstring bag and secured it to his person along with his other things. A bit cumbersome, but traveling with it served another, more practical purpose. Should the hunt ever go against him, he'd arranged for his soul to escape into the mirror until a suitable body presented itself for possession. It was risky, a spell that could only be practiced once.

It had taken too long to find a worthy adversary and it seemed as though not just his stomach, but all his organs grumbled with the terrible, aching hunger he'd grown accustomed to—a part of the curse he would never forgive. Even his muscles quivered with the need for sustenance and his mouth watered, not with a longing for the rabbits and quail he was once able to roast over an open fire, but for the blood of an enemy that was completely unaware of his existence. For now.

He raised his hands in the air, threw his head back and screamed. A guttural, anguished howl of deprivation. Cruelly deprived of his home and of his nature when those who did not understand him deemed his self-education a criminal activity. The experiment with the goblin's heart had been a stunning success, but also the beginning of his troubles.

Foley doused the embers, gathered three clay jars that had been carefully tucked away in the trunk, and climbed down the ladder. After a short hike to yet another cemetery—the area around his cave being conveniently crowded with dead pioneers—he crouched and felt along the fence until his arm sank elbow deep into the wet grass.

Touching the necklace again, he grinned with both rows of his teeth. While perfecting the necromantic arts, he'd learned to infuse it with blood from each hunt. It had cost him precious beads to build a small army of undead soldiers, but they were a necessary, if not profitable, investment.

It would not please the locals that there were little hovels hiding corpses that would not properly rot outside the cemetery gates of every town Foley had ever visited, but it pleased him. Each of his jars held the spirit of one of their own people. Spirits captured and trapped, driven mad by their imprisonment, unable to proceed into whatever afterlife awaited them.

The smell of tobacco wafted up as he opened the pots one by one. To summon the shades from their vessels he lit the contents with a match, shook it out quickly, and then waited for them to rise within the smoke. By this time, he had little patience for the complaints of the misty ghosts that soon circled around him. They were angry spirits, restrained by the demands of their warden, the first of which being that they return to their bodies lest he smash the jars and leave them in the ether. So, they did as they were told.

Foley shook a small branch of yew pine, sprinkled its needles over the mossy patch of earth and tugged on the worn-out shoe of one of his painstakingly handmade ghouls. Guided by the scent of the yew, the mists hovered low and slipped into the mottled noses of three emaciated creatures, once men, who crawled, reluctantly, out of their shallow mass grave. At first stumbling about in confusion, the ghouls soon recognized their master and danced with desperation. Dirty and tattered, they too were hungry.

* * *

The ramshackle construction outside of Fort Verde could hardly be called a town but the civilians in residence had managed to cobble together a general store, a hotel-brothel with a restaurant, and a post office where one could also send a telegram. There was no boardwalk to speak of so Jess stood in the mud frowning as he read the wire from Clemente's son, Juan Hinojosa. Juan's promising lead had run dry, and he had no news of Adam's whereabouts. He suggested heading south toward Phoenix.

Jess crumpled the paper and turned abruptly from the window, just in time to see Dusty Dorman duck behind the hotel.

As expected, the Marshal was waiting for him when Jess entered the alley. His eyes darted around to make sure they were alone and then he said, "Don't tell me you came to this shit hole seeking out more of my company."

"If you must know, I seek the company of an imaginative little whore named Theresa," Dusty countered, "but first I have a message for you...Jess Carson."

Jess narrowed his eyes and let his fingers hover over his pistol. He was fast but he doubted that he could best Dusty. Marshal Dorman had lived an exceedingly long life for a lawman and that was no accident. As such it wasn't worth it to try keeping up the lie—he had too much respect for Dusty to insult him like that anyway.

It was just as well since Jess had decided that whether he found Adam or not, he would die before letting himself hang for the crime that awful bitch committed.

Dusty wasn't particularly worried about getting killed either—he didn't consider himself to be that lucky. Besides, he'd worked with James/Jess often enough to know that he was a relatively decent man at heart. Still, he never took his eyes off Jess's gun hand. A lefty was tricky–had to be–but the Marshal was ready.

He gave Jess a thin smile and said, "It may please you to know that you and your friend are no longer wanted for robbery and murder."

Jess gaped at him. "Why?"

Dusty made the slightest of shrugs. "I'm told that it was all some sort of misunderstanding, but Jess Carson and Adam Colter are no longer my problems, so I really don't give a damn."

"You're lying."

He'd been on the run for a long time and, as the Marshal had anticipated, Jess would not be easily convinced. Even if they hadn't been cleared of wrongdoing, the details of that case had bothered Dusty from the beginning. The warrant was vague: two men and a woman who had robbed a bank in Flagstaff. Before he died, the man they allegedly killed had admitted to shooting one of the robbers in the chest but could not describe any of them.

"Believe what you want," Dusty said, "but I'm not going to arrest you today," he tilted his head at Jess's gun hand, adding, "unless you do something stupid."

"What about the cashier she killed?"

Aha. The Marshal could demand more information about the woman, but it would only be to satisfy his own curiosity and that was not what he was being paid to do. "I suppose you can feel guilty about it if you want to," he offered, "but I'm here because Mark Chisolm hired me to give you this."

He held up a tri-folded piece of paper, then lifted a rock with the toe of his boot, put the paper under the rock and slowly began to walk backward away from Jess.

His grin widened as he said, "Now that I'm flush with *my* earnings, I'll bet Theresa will be as happy to see me as I am to see her."

"Who the hell is Mark Chisolm?" Jess approached the rock and stared at it for several seconds before reaching for the paper.

"You'll find out."

Jess read the letter twice and then looked up, calling out to Dusty, "Do you know where I can find Adam?"

After everything he imagined that Jess Carson had gone through, Dusty found himself genuinely disappointed to be the bearer of bad news as he turned away and said, "No son, I do not."

Chapter Three

Jess took his time on the ride to Prescott while contemplating the mysterious letter, certain that he'd never met anyone named Mark Chisolm and slightly unnerved by how much the man seemed to know about him. Still, he learned right away that the Chisolm letter would open quite a few doors.

In town, he wandered around the train station for a while, not quite sure who or what to look for. He didn't find Chisolm, but after showing the letter to the ticket clerk, everyone else he met seemed happy to offer their assistance. A little too happy. Jess was led to the livery car, where Pepper boarded in fine style for the journey. Though it wasn't much, his saddle bags contained everything he owned, including his rifle, and he was loathe to leave his horse or his belongings for very long; but he gathered what would fit in the pockets of his long duster coat and covered up everything else.

Briefly resting his forehead against hers, he reassured an anxious Pepper and was then introduced to the Station Master who escorted Jess to his office for further instruction. The Station Master was a short, round, affable man who called himself The Broker.

"I make arrangements," he explained, "complicated arrangements, for your more complicated individuals." The Broker looked up and, giving Jess the onceover, added, "You must be a lawman—the most complicated sort by far."

"Bounty hunter these days," Jess clarified, "better pay."

The Broker nodded as if that explained everything, but then peered over his glasses and said, "Shorter life expectancy I imagine."

"To be honest," he admitted, "I am surprised I've made it this far."

Jess had felt an odd obligation to Mark Chisolm for taking him and Adam off the 'Wanted' list and had blindly followed the letter's instructions, both out of morbid curiosity and with the hope that the mission would somehow get him closer to finding his brother. But he didn't like being confused and scowled as he looked around the office for clues.

Sensing his waning patience, The Broker took a set of keys from his belt and motioned for Jess to follow him to the back of the room. There he used three different keys to unlock a narrow, floor to ceiling cabinet which contained a long slender item that sat alone on the wooden shelf.

It was a little over a foot in length, wrapped tightly in at least two layers of brown paper and secured with plenty of string. Jess could have sworn he caught The Broker emitting a short sigh of relief once it was handed over to him.

Mark's letter said that Jess was to safeguard and deliver an item of great importance, so he had assumed it would be a trunk or a payroll box of some kind.

"This is it?" He asked.

The Broker nodded. "Mr. Chisolm will meet you at the station in Phoenix and explain everything—

assuming that you and the package arrive safely."

The ominous statement registered with Jess, but he didn't respond to it. Safety was not something he'd ever taken for granted, and he was quite sure both Mark Chisolm and The Broker understood that about him.

With that in mind, he reminded him, "I get paid up front."

Nodding again, The Broker returned to his desk and produced an envelope—thicker than Jess had expected—from the drawer.

Jess tucked the money away and examined the package. It wasn't very heavy, but it was awkward and would draw attention, so he redistributed the contents of his coat to hide it as well as he could in the largest pocket.

"One last thing—your ticket." Now free of the package, The Broker seemed anxious to rid himself of Jess as well and ushered him to the door. "I don't wish to appear rude, but I have another appointment."

Not that he would have recognized him, but Jess didn't notice Mark Chisolm slipping into The Broker's office after he left. His attention had been captured by the sound of a woman's voice echoing over the din of the crowded station.

"No sir, I'm sure you are a fine gentleman, but as I said, I simply need one ticket, one way, to Phoenix," she insisted, pushing her money across the counter. The woman turned away from the amorous clerk, clearly fatigued from the uncomfortable exchange. Still, she smiled at her ticket as if it were the key to her prison cell.

After carefully tucking it in the drawstring purse secured around her wrist, she situated her ruby-colored coat over her forearm, adjusted her hat, and picked up her tapestry bag. She would have marched triumphantly toward the platform had not the back hem of her dress, made from the same dark red calico as her purse, caught on the head of a nail protruding from floorboard. With a sigh, she dropped her things and attempted to free herself.

As he approached her, Jess suddenly became aware of his own dusty travel clothes and gave his vest a quick brush with his hands before offering his assistance.

"That's very kind of you, but I—" Her voice caught in her throat as she looked up into the warmest brown eyes she'd ever seen. They had a heavy-lidded, mournful slope to them, but still shone with amusement at her predicament. She also noticed the slightly unnatural angle of his right arm and how, ignoring her objections, he used his left hand to carefully pull the thread away from the nail.

"I won't tear it," he promised, his mouth twisting slightly as he tried not to laugh.

While grappling with the knot, mindful of not exposing her legs to passersby, he spied the boots on her feet, more suitable for riding a horse than a train. Then, as he finally untethered her from the nail, his fingers grazed the hem of the pants she wore underneath the outfit.

She caught him staring and fluffed the skirt around her. "I'm sure you're one of the best of men, but even some of them have trouble controlling their baser instincts out in the wild. I realize it's unconventional, but you must understand that a woman can never be too careful."

Her solution wasn't likely to be much of a deterrent,

but she was traveling alone, and he admired her intrepid spirit. Lowering his voice, he leaned close to her ear and said, "Your saucy secret is safe with me."

Just then the Conductor walked through the station, his voice booming that the train to Phoenix would be delayed for two hours while debris was cleared from the tracks near Black Canyon City.

"Dammit," she swore and then pressed her lips together, embarrassed by the unladylike utterance.

He laughed out loud and agreed, "My sentiments exactly."

Jess knew of a small restaurant nearby and though in his notes the place was infamous for its terrible, often dangerous food, the last time he was in Prescott, they'd managed to make him a decent cup of coffee. He wondered if the unconventional lady would think it inappropriate to accompany him but as he mentally fumbled with the words to ask her, a young girl of about twelve years old ran up and grabbed her hand.

"Mademoiselle...Mademoiselle," the girl panted, "you must come...you must come and read the tarot cards."

The woman knelt to be eye level with the girl and said, "I'm leaving on the train soon."

The girl shook her head vigorously. "Si vous plait," as she caught her breath, she began to explain, "Madame Danwell spoke so highly of you that Madame Auclair begs you to come and read for her." The girl shook a small pouch full of coins at her and added, "more when you help...je promets."

"Tarot cards?" Still smiling, Jess arched an eyebrow and asked, "Are you psychic or something?"

"It's not that simple," she lifted her chin, "but most

people are psychic on some level."

He doubted that or he would have found Adam a long time ago.

"Madamoiselle," The girl hopped from foot to foot, terrified of her punishment if she returned home alone.

"You have the time," Jess said with a wink, "it's almost like...your destiny or something."

He was mocking her but, she didn't take offense. The insults he had likely endured in his lifetime because of that arm would have been much more severe than his own playful teasing. Besides, people mocked her for any number of reasons, her uncanny skills not the worst of them. Had her financial circumstances been different she would have chosen another interim profession but that was not the case–not yet anyway–so for the time being she'd put what she'd always referred to as her *sensitivities* to work by reading the cards.

She returned his contagious grin as the girl dragged her away, and called out, "Thank you for your help!"

Jess had met mediums before, usually crooked frauds and thieves. Certainly, none so pretty as the lady who wore pants. It occurred to him as he watched her disappear around the corner that he hadn't learned her name.

"Damn."

* * *

Madame Auclair paced so erratically in front of the fireplace that they could hear the rustling of her silk petticoats before the young girl even ushered Cory to the sitting room. Nearby was a tall, thin man doing his best to comfort her while he teetered on his heels with a drink in his hand.

In broken English, the girl had explained during the walk, or rather run, to the house that Suzannah Auclair believed she was being haunted by her fiancé's late wife, whose ghost was seemingly opposed to the marriage.

The girl, wise beyond her years, felt it prudent to mention that Suzannah was from Atlanta and had been orphaned during the war. She was young, adventurous, and rich. Cory had already heard the gossip in town. Suzannah's fiancé, Alain Auclair, made the decision to move them to Arizona before the wedding based on a potential mining investment; but so eager was he to marry that he'd convinced Suzannah to begin using his name as she infiltrated Prescott society, such as it was.

Though outside the early spring air had a crisp chill to it, inside the Auclair home was stifling. Cory tugged at the neck of her blouse as beads of sweat instantly formed along her hairline. The girl removed her outer layers, tossed them casually across the back of a chair, and gestured for Cory to do the same.

"Keep them close," she advised, assigning Cory's things to the other arm of the chair.

"Please! Do sit down right here," Suzannah demanded, waving her hand over a small but elegant round table near the open window. It was only just large enough for the two chairs she'd positioned on either side of it, and there wasn't much room for Cory to spread out her tarot cards due to the placement of a large, framed photograph in the center.

"Ahem." The tall man pursed his lips at the bride to be, who promptly gathered herself.

"Forgive me, Miss Lindsay," she said, "and thank you ever so much for coming as quickly as you did. I've prepared this space for us to work."

Suzannah was an agitated little whirlwind with the palest, most delicate skin Cory had ever seen. Everything about her was fair, even her sage green eyes. As she flittered about, whisps of baby fine wheat blonde hair escaped from underneath an intricately braided attachment. It was pinned to a bun that had been twisted with her own hair at the back of her head. Though it was lovely, the thick hairpiece looked as if it might crumple the young woman's slender neck under its weight.

Cory had been anticipating nothing more than pre-wedding jitters and maybe a bit of insecurity about the groom's feelings. Both could be alleviated by drawing a few cards and offering some encouraging words, but the intensity of Suzannah's fear gave her pause.

"Of course." Cory picked up the frame and examined the photograph of a couple she assumed to be Alain Auclair and his dead first wife. The photograph was not of a good quality but based on the woman's dress, it must have been taken on their wedding day.

Perspiration trickled down her back and her vision blurred as the walls of the room seemed to close in all around. In her mind, Cory could clearly see a woman standing in a citrus grove with Alain in her arms. It was not the woman in the picture, and it was not Suzannah.

Chapter Four

"Yvonne suffered a tragic accident two years ago," the tall man explained in a French accent, snapping Cory's attention back to the people in the room.

"Yvonne?" Cory fished a handkerchief from her pocket and dabbed at her forehead.

When she blinked at him, he bowed slightly at the waist and added, "Apologies, Yvonne was my brother's first wife and I am René Auclair, at your service."

"Alain's younger brother," Suzannah clarified, "in town for our wedding. And this is Chloé, their baby sister."

"I am no baby." Chloé crossed her arms and sat down hard in one of the chairs at the little table.

Suzannah ignored the girl's protest and began to pace again. "I had thought that Yvonne would leave me alone when we moved so far away, but she continues to torture me."

A sudden chill swept through the room just then, leaving ice crystals across Cory's sweat dampened skin and sending shiver after shiver down her spine.

Chloé handed Cory her coat and said, "Now you see?"

René moved to Cory's side, his eyes hardening as they darted around the room. Exhaling in a misty cloud, he asked, "Are you alright?"

"I'm fine," Cory said, though she was anything but.

The scent of lime wafted through the room on a strong breeze that fluttered the curtains and tipped a vase of flowers from a side table next to the sofa. They all jumped as the vase shattered, and Suzannah instinctively reached out to box Chloé's ears.

The girl executed a practiced dodge, wailing, "It was not me!"

Cory stared at the broken vase, despairing slightly. Yvonne's ghost could cause her to miss the train, and she would have to stay in Prescott, reading cards and evading the Propriety Guild until she made enough money for another ticket.

"Shall we do a séance?" Suzannah whisked the curtains closed.

Cory had received hundreds of visions in her lifetime, and she was, on occasion, perceptive to the activities of the spirit world, but her few past attempts at summoning them directly had been failures. As such if she'd ever performed a séance for pay, it would have been all for show. There were some people, parents mostly, who really wanted to believe and though they were willing to pay extra for that show, she refused them all.

Sensing an energy or a presence was one thing but without the help of a witch, it was rare that real spirits were able to expose themselves to the living. Still, there was no doubt that someone else was in that house with them. The Auclairs had evidently been getting quite a show for free.

She sighed, "No need for a séance today, I'm afraid."

The air grew close around them, heavy with angst

and desperation. Temperature changes and broken vases were not the work of a jealous poltergeist, they were the tactics of someone with a message—or a warning.

"Listen to what people say and pay attention to your surroundings," Cory's mother had told her when she was a little girl, "the smallest bit of sensitivity goes a long way."

Cory was taught to look for the messages in her visions. Her mother believed that they were special women, chosen to receive direct communication from God; but Cory found it inconvenient that the communication was only one way and often wished God had given her a more practical gift.

Since coming out west, she'd used her annoying— often frightening—gift for survival. People who'd given up everything back east for a better life in the desert frequently found that what they ended up with was more difficult and more perilous than anything they'd ever imagined, and they were desperate to learn about their future.

They were willing to share their most intimate details, and it was easy for her to offer advice that she could credit to the tarot cards. She was quite proud of the money she'd earned by telling people what they needed to hear.

While Cory might exaggerate the power of the tarot on occasion, she hadn't ever considered herself a fraud—not really. She understood people. And the visions, if unpredictable, were real.

The vision that began when she walked in the door of the Auclair home still played in the back of her mind, demanding her full attention; just like Suzannah.

"Miss Lindsay?"

Cory took off her gloves and held Suzannah's freezing hands in her own. "How is Yvonne torturing you?" She asked.

"Oh," Suzannah covered her face with her hands, "she comes to me in my dreams."

Inwardly, Cory breathed a sigh of relief. Even the most awful dreams could often be explained quickly, one simply needed all the details.

A curious Chloé perched on the arm of a dark blue velvet sofa and pretended to smoke a cigarette with her frosty breath.

René pulled the chairs out for Cory and Suzannah to be seated. He'd berated his soon to be sister-in-law for summoning a charlatan, but this medium was nothing like he'd expected. To study the lovely woman was no hardship, and he could find no fakery in her movements. She'd witnessed their unsettling happenings but controlled her fear while making every attempt to soothe Suzannah. The wildness of the west had not found a way to crush her spirit, and he no longer cared whether she was a fraud. He wanted to learn everything about her.

Cory took a deck of tarot cards from the outside pocket of her tapestry bag, shuffled the deck and laid a three-card spread face down between the two women.

She turned over the first card and said to Suzannah, "Judgment."

"Too much light, René," Chloé complained, thinking that if they were to be haunted by her dead sister-in-law, the room should have a more ghostly aesthetic.

When he moved to close the curtains on the other

window, Cory shook her head, "Please don't." She gave Chloé an apologetic nod, but the brightness gave her the illusion of warmth in the room.

"Tell me about the dreams."

"Yvonne smells of rotten citrus and drags a nightgown behind her as she walks. She screams and flies at me. She tries to suffocate me, and I wake unable to breathe." Silent tears ran down Suzannah's cheeks as she spoke.

Cory's brow furrowed. The second card she turned up was the seven of swords. She looked up at Suzannah and said, "Betrayal."

"This gown..." she continued, trying to keep the impatience out of her voice.

"It's white with a blue ribbon woven through the neckline," Suzannah blurted.

Chloé stood and bounced up and down on her toes. "Oui, oui, I have seen this gown," she said, "in Alain's study."

René took her roughly by the arm. "Why have you been snooping around in there?"

"To look at pictures of Mama." She jerked free of his grasp. "When Alain is out."

René sighed. He'd been surprised that Suzannah found Yvonne's wedding photo, but the devious Chloé would have shown her his brother's hiding place. There were few photos of the family, and it was true that Alain kept most of them locked away.

Chloé sprinted out of the room and returned moments later carrying a delicate cotton nightgown perfectly matching Suzannah's description.

Suzannah leapt from the sofa and backed away with a shriek. She would have set her expensive skirts aflame had René not moved himself between her and the fireplace.

"Where did you get that?" Cory took the gown from the girl, but she needn't have bothered asking since the vision of its owner overtook her senses once again. In her mind, she observed the same unfamiliar woman in the citrus grove behind that very house, wearing the gown. The woman pressed herself against Alain, who whispered her name over and over as he kissed her.

Cory opened her eyes and asked René directly, "Who is Amelia?"

"Amelia?" Suzannah did not give him a chance to respond. "Amelia is their cousin. We are bringing her here from Charleston after the wedding."

"Suzannah," Cory said, taking her hands again, "this gown belongs to Amelia."

The group went silent for a few seconds and then Suzannah turned to René. "Amelia. She is your cousin?"

Cory noted that for the first time since she'd arrived, René put down his drink.

"We have no *cousin* Amelia, but," he avoided her gaze, "Alain once courted a woman with that name when we were much younger."

Suzannah went to the window and absently ran her fingers along the sash, quietly fusing all that René left unsaid with Cory's vision and the information in the cards.

After several minutes, she called out to Yvonne, "Is Amelia his mistress?"

The flames shot high in the fireplace, spraying sparks across the hearth which René stomped out before they reached the rug.

Suzannah turned to him, asking, "If he truly loves

this Amelia woman, why wouldn't Alain marry her?"

Chloé ran her fingers along the sleeve of the simple threadbare gown and said what the others had been thinking, "She has no fortune."

"Please." Suzannah tapped the third card.

Cory turned it over, looked up and whispered, "Justice."

Suzannah put her hands to her throat as she tried to come to grips with the fact that the rich, handsome Alain Auclair, the man with whom she had shared her body and intended to share her life, had likely murdered his first wife for her money. As if to confirm their suspicions, the petals on the floor wilted away from their stems and the dried flowers swirled around the room in a fragrant dust devil, briefly engulfing Suzannah before catching the breeze and floating out the window.

Alain had returned early from what turned out to be a surprisingly productive business meeting and was feeling quite self-assured until he spied Chloé running down the hall with Amelia's nightgown. He would beat the traitorous girl later, but for a long while he stood just outside the sitting room, listening as a stranger unveiled his secrets.

A bolt of fury shot through him, but he calmed almost as quickly, knowing that Suzannah carried her own great secret. While she was unlikely to call off the wedding, her knowledge of Amelia's true identity complicated matters unnecessarily. There was nothing he could do with his fiancé except wait for her emotions to subside, but he stormed out to the courtyard to intercept the psychic, whom he would deal with swiftly.

Cradling the unnoticeable bump in her belly, Suzannah whispered, "It cannot be true." Lifting her eyes skyward, she begged the spirit of Yvonne, "Say it is not true."

The wedding photo frame fell forward, then levitated before crashing down over and over as if someone unseen was smashing it against the table. It was one hell of an answer to the question, Cory thought, and no surprise.

Suzannah didn't flinch at the ruckus, only stared down at the broken pieces. Cory worried that, fragile as she was, she might break as well, but then the young woman stood up straight and pulled her shoulders back into a posture that revealed she was quite a bit taller than Cory originally thought.

Suzannah had made herself small in stature, light on education, and deferential to Alain's opinions, even though she had many of her own. In truth, she was rather fascinated by the topics that he insisted were of no concern to her. She knew deep down that all women should concern themselves with money and politics as such things dictated every aspect of their lives. Still, she'd made herself as tiny and unobtrusive as possible for him.

But even her voice deepened as Suzannah's innocence appeared to shatter along with the picture frame. The naïve nineteen-year-old bride was, before their eyes, replaced with a more practical woman who began to swiftly take stock of her unfortunate situation.

"He might try to kill me like, I assume, he killed Yvonne," she said, turning again to René. "There was an endowment from her family, was there not?"

René nodded. "A modest amount. Enough to

finance your move to Arizona and—"

"And his investment in the mine," Suzannah interrupted, "imagine what he could do with *my* inheritance."

"Wives die all the time," she said to herself, tapping a finger on her chin, "but then again so do husbands, don't they? Husbands who go down to the mines often die in accidents. You read about it in the papers every day."

Cory felt guilty about having to abandon the family so quickly after sharing such bad news; and she was uncomfortable with where Suzannah's thoughts were headed. Arranging an accident of that sort was perilous at best.

She leaned in close and held Suzannah's gaze. "Haven't you any knowledge of herbs?" She asked, wondering if the young woman might possess enough information to solve her problems by more delicate means.

Suzannah knew nothing about such things and cursed herself for having airs over the women back in Atlanta who could have taught her, who tried to teach her. "Can you help me?"

She could. Cory had fantasized many times of becoming a self-made widow, but while he was cold and hateful, her ex-husband was not dangerous. In Suzannah's situation, she could advocate for a woman's self-defense, but not, as it would have been in her own case, spiteful murder. Even so, there were many nights when she lulled herself to sleep with happy thoughts of his untimely demise.

Her shoulders lifted with tension. She could teach the girl, but if she did not catch that train, she would never be free of her own miserable past.

René caught her glancing at the clock on the mantel and intervened, "I'm afraid we have kept you for too long," he said, before ordering Chloé to fetch her some travel provisions.

"I wish I didn't have to go," Cory said honestly.

"What I don't know I will learn," Suzannah assured her, and with a sly nod she added, "I will keep you informed of my progress."

"Please be careful," Cory begged her and then turned to René, "You will look after her?"

He nodded. There had been many times over the years when René would have killed the wicked Alain himself, and though he was not yet convinced of her resolve in the matter, he would not only protect Suzannah, but he would also assist her if necessary.

Chloé returned promptly with a little round tin containing two fluffy biscuits slathered with butter and jam. She'd even included an orange from the grove.

"You are too kind after I've caused you so much pain," Cory protested, but Suzannah flipped over one more card and then gave her a bright smile.

"The sun," Cory said.

"My path is clear, and I owe it to you."

Cory had her doubts, but Suzannah was convinced that she had saved her life and, true to her word, she paid handsomely for her services before asking René to see her out.

As they reached the gate at the end of the courtyard, Alain lurched from the trees, grabbed Cory by the back of the neck and dragged her to the side of the house.

"Stupid witch," he hissed in her ear, "you've brought a whole lot of trouble down on me."

René relished every opportunity to fight his brother, but before he had the chance to make a move, Mark Chisolm stepped behind them out of nowhere and pushed a pistol to Alain's temple.

Cory yelped as the grip tightened on her neck.

"I think you'll not shoot me in my own house," Alain argued.

René leaned against the trunk of an orange tree and folded his arms across his chest. "Yvonne paid for this house, no?"

"Let her go." Mark pulled the hammer back. "Now."

Alain shoved Cory at René and swung his fist around wildly in Mark's direction, but he could not connect before Mark's pistol came down across the back of his head. He fell to his knees and then on his face, blacking out entirely.

"Get her on the train," Mark ordered René.

The shadow that the sun cast over Mark's hat hid his face from view and the long coat he wore concealed the rest of his clothing so that Cory could barely tell that he was human. She reached out to thank him, but René held her back.

"Who are you?" She was desperate to know the rest of their story.

With his gun still aimed at Alain's head, Mark growled at her to go.

René was maddeningly quiet on the walk to the train station, and Cory's mind was reeling. She was no stranger to cold-hearted family members, but the Auclairs were positively ruthless. Even little Chloé seemed unmoved by Suzannah's hastily formed revenge plot.

"If she kills your brother—" Cory started.

"Alain's well-being has never been a concern of mine," he seethed.

"But you promised to protect her."

"Of course I will."

"Who was that man?" She pressed.

"No, chére," René insisted, "no more questions today."

Chapter Five

Pepper reared back as Foley pressed against her flank. She recognized the sickening sensation triggered by his presence near the river and tossed her head about, frantically searching for Jess. Foley laughed and stomped his foot at her before leaving the livery car with a whistle on his lips.

Always there was jubilance when worthy prey was discovered, but the battle would feel empty if the chase was unrewarding. The true thrill of the hunt was dependent upon the collection of intimate details, emotional threads that could be pulled from the bounty hunter along the way. The loss of a beloved horse would certainly provoke him, but he would soon uncover that one detail, the perfect motivation for a fight.

The self-control required to gather such details was not a gift that Foley came by naturally. Disregarding his violent instincts often caused him to lose focus, but he was determined this time to ignore the hunger pangs, certain that the reward in the end would be as satisfying as it would be delicious.

He settled in between the engine and the postal car to wait for the train's departure while the three ghouls disbursed themselves, hanging on the outside of various cars, drooling with impatience as they spied on the passengers.

* * *

René was reluctant to let her go but as instructed, he escorted Cory to the passenger car without another word spoken. Despite his stoic demeanor, he flinched at the cool breeze that wafted across his right side when she moved away from him to climb the steps. The warmth of a woman on his arm was a luxury he rarely allowed himself and he silently cursed Mark Chisolm for leaving one so special in his charge. One he would not soon forget.

Cory was positively distracted by his seeming indifference as she boarded, trying to parse out the events of her afternoon spent with the Auclair family.

Though she had, on occasion, been witness to a wandering spirit, she'd never before walked into a room with one already there. If they had a purpose at all, ghosts tended to reveal themselves more subtly, but Yvonne was anything but. *Poor Yvonne.*

Suzannah did not really need those cards, did she? Cory wished their time hadn't been cut so short, convinced that she and the young woman would have become fast friends. There was no knowing what Alain might try to do now that his secret was out. René's protective nature comforted her somewhat and though she had been literally dragged into the family fray, the whole thing left her feeling like she might have been less than qualified to step into their business. Only time would tell if she had truly saved Suzannah's life.

For a brief moment Cory pined for the family she left behind but when comparing her people to the Auclairs, there were quite a few unsettling similarities and decided it best not to dwell on them. The ride to

Phoenix was a long one and she would have used the time to contemplate her future, but the unknown made her anxious. Since it had all been unknown once she first stepped foot in Arizona it was better just to wait and see. In an attempt to divert her attention for a while she pulled a slim volume from her pocket.

"Watcha readin'?"

Cory had no sooner opened the book when she felt the stranger's hot, rancid breath in her ear.

"Is it the Bible? I figure a mature woman like you for a Sunday School teacher."

She moved as far away as she could, pressing her back against the window as he leaned farther over the seat.

"I am not," she said.

Chunks of tobacco were caked onto his teeth and large droplets of his sweat soaked into her skirt as he reached over and grabbed the book. "Black Beet—"

"It's called Black Beauty," she corrected, snatching it back. He could think her "mature", but she would not let him think that he could steal her things right out of her hands.

He pumped his eyebrows at her. "Who's the beauty?"

"It's a story about the life of a horse named Black Beauty." She bowed her head and pretended to continue reading, but he didn't take the hint.

"A horse's life ain't that interesting."

"The horse tells the story, and it is very interesting."

"I never met a horse who could tell a story."

She blinked at him. "Sir, a woman wrote the book about how we should treat horses with kindness, and each chapter is about an incident in Black Beauty's life.

You see, he was born on a farm but then he was handled cruelly and forced to pull cabs in London, and then..."

Jess smiled, watching the exchange from the back of the car. He'd readied himself to intervene, but she out-chatted her harasser to the point where he lost interest, shaking his head at Jess as he passed by.

Cory sighed with nervous relief when he left, and her fingers trembled so badly as she turned the pages that she had to lay the book in her lap. Unwilling to burden her with further unwanted attention, Jess eased himself onto a bench across the aisle, two rows behind.

Though preferable to a stagecoach, it had been Jess's experience that trains were hot, crowded and boisterous. So, aside from the accompanying stench that filtered through the cars, he was pleased to learn that their train was transporting a load of mainly livestock and mail with few passengers on board—not even a dining car.

From a seat to himself, he studied the woman. She wore her rich brown hair in a braided chignon, but several tendrils had escaped since he'd last seen her. He found it charming the way the curls framed her face but then noticed some bruising on the back of her neck and a small tear at the top of her sleeve. *What happened after the little girl hurried her away?*

He stood to go to her, demanding answers, but sat back down when she laid her head against the window and closed her eyes. She seemed alright and whatever had happened was only part of what would be a long tiring day, so he decided to let her rest.

From his post near the engine, Foley's skin prickled

with a sudden and surprising sense of yearning emanating from the bounty hunter. The source, he discovered, was a woman in a handmade red dress, asleep in a seat by herself. Foley stood between the cars and tried to slow his breathing. Jess Carson was so close that his fingers twitched to be around his neck, but the woman...she was a detail that could not be ignored.

Asleep in her seat, Cory dreamed of the man who had released her skirt from the nail. He and a dark-haired man she didn't recognize laughed together as they rode their horses side by side along the banks of a river she'd never been to.

Himself wide awake, Jess shifted in his seat and rubbed at his ribcage. Often, he felt pain in the place where he'd been shot but this was an unfamiliar pressure that mingled with a dank odor and an oppressive gloom that just then seemed to fill the entire car.

Soon, an unnaturally tall man passed him in the aisle and paused to lean over the woman. The man was well dressed but grotesquely thin and his fancy hat could not hide the thin strands of long gray hair that hung down his shoulders in greasy clumps.

Cory whined softly as Foley reached across her seat, using a boney finger to mark her forehead with a bit of cemetery dirt. He'd mixed it with valerian that grew near the children's graves, and it made him smile to think that the cemetery was better stocked for his purposes than most general stores.

Jess rose again to go to her but was stopped by a powerful dust devil that kicked up out of nowhere, and when it cleared the strange man was gone.

Foley's dirty potion dissolved into Cory's skin and

soon, the river in her dream began to freeze over and the dark-haired man's horse fell behind. He and the brown eyed man called to one another, but the ice crept out of the river and grew between the the two men until only the one with dark hair was visible.

Though she hadn't seen herself in the dream, he turned in the saddle as if looking right at her. He seemed so sad that, out of character, she whispered a prayer for him.

"Be careful, Miss," he warned, before riding off in the opposite direction, "the Devil can hear your prayers too."

Her eyes flew open and as she caught her breath, Cory looked up to see the brown eyed man smiling down at her. She was sincerely grateful that Jess apparently did not chew tobacco as there was none stuck to his teeth. What she couldn't have known is that he'd always had a distaste for it since Walter Sallow had spit the brown sludge all over their house before crushing his arm and killing his grandfather.

"Everything alright?" He asked.

She nodded and looked away to hide her blush, not trusting her words after dreaming about him—in front of him.

He tipped his hat with a wink and as he continued down the aisle, she thought to herself that a man with such eyes must have a great many stories to tell. If her disturbing dream was at all prophetic, a fair number of those stories were far from pleasant. Still, she caught herself yearning to hear them all.

Before returning to her book, she noticed as he left, a sign above him and the passageway that read, "Proceed Here Safely". Of course, it was only reminding passengers to use caution between the cars, but she was overcome with the embarrassing desire to follow him out. Only once before had she seen a sign that elicited such a powerful impulse. It was in the church on her wedding day, and it read, "This Way Out." She had ignored her instincts then, to her detriment.

He was reluctant to leave her alone, but Jess needed some fresh air and a good stretch of his legs—as good a stretch as the narrow passageways would allow. They'd been traveling for hours and the strange events of the day, let alone the past few minutes, had him rattled.

The air turned out to be filled with smoke and cinders from the stack but though the noise outside was deafening, Jess was grateful to have a private spot in the gangway to sort things out.

Men didn't just disappear. It had been an odd thing, but most likely the train somehow kicked up the dust and his tired mind was playing tricks with him. Still, he would keep an eye out for the gangly man and learn just what he was doing on that train and with that woman.

Jess resituated the ill-shaped package in his coat pocket and decided to check on Pepper in the livery car. First, he readied himself for a quick conversation with the pretty lady in the red dress. He would remember her fondly when they parted ways in Phoenix, and he wanted to know her name.

Foley laid flat on top of the passenger car, leaning as far

as he dared to look in the window, making sure the bounty hunter and the woman were in position. He had a feeling that his targets were survivors at heart, but if their bodies were killed, the hunt would have to start over and there was no time for that. Even so, the risk was part of the rush, and his pulse quickened at the thought of what was about to happen.

He made a sharp whistle and the ghoul waiting on the ladder sprang into action, running across the top of the car to meet the brakeman who would undoubtedly be there soon.

Foley gave one last glance through the window, smiled and said, "Jess Carson, it is time for us to be properly introduced."

"God dammit!" The engineer spied the cloud of dust emerging from the trees surrounding at least two horsemen.

He shouted, "Get the conductor!", and the flagman sprinted through the cars.

When they began their journey, the engineer had expected robbers to come for the safe in the mail car, but just a few minutes earlier he'd thought to himself that they were finally close enough to Phoenix to be safe.

Cursing his overconfidence, he yelled to his fireman for more speed before spotting the damage to the tracks on the bridge. Gaping out the window he swore again. Up ahead was a thirty-foot ravine crossed by a narrow truss bridge where a section of the ties had been ripped away.

"Those fools cleared the debris but didn't fix the

track!"

He couldn't have known that it was not robbers headed toward them on horseback but two more of Foley's ghouls who, hours before, had damaged the tracks and intercepted the repair crew. What remained of the crew's bodies lay in pieces, barely hidden by the trees.

There was a strangled cry behind him, and the engineer turned just in time to see Foley grab the fireman by the neck and throw him out the door.

"What the hell are you doing?"

In lieu of an answer, Foley lifted his palm and blew a handful of the potion made from powdered bones into his face. The irritation instantly clogged the engineer's tear ducts. His hands flew to his burning eyes then grasped at his throat. His tongue thickened and turned black, choking him as it swelled. The bloody tears that managed to escape down his cheeks were nothing more than liquid poison soaking into his blue lips, and soon his tongue grew so big that it pushed out his false teeth just before he toppled over dead at Foley's feet.

Chapter Six

"Robbers!" The flagman burst into the caboose where the conductor was settled in at his desk, going over the route while the brakeman made them coffee. "They've torn up the tracks!"

"Stay calm." The conductor squeezed the brakeman's arm and ordered, "Get up there, Archie."

Archie was a gentle giant most of the time but, as his wife's mean drunk of a brother could attest to, a barely controlled temper simmered underneath his outwardly good nature. He curled his hands into fists a few times before grabbing his club, smiling at the thought of catching a no-good thief upside the head with it.

"They'll have guns, Arch," the conductor warned him.

Archie flipped his club, touched the brim of his cap with the thick end in a sort of salute and then swung out the door and up the ladder to do his job.

The brake wheel atop the mail car behind the engine was stuck, so Archie shoved in his club and cranked down on the wheel as hard as he could. Though he crouched low, the wind and the rocking of the speeding train kept him off balance and he never saw the ghoul approaching from behind before it bit down on his shoulder. Archie whirled the club around, catching the ghoul under the chin with a satisfying crack, but then teetered and fell forward on his chest.

He'd never seen one before but the ghoul, pale with blood red eyes, mangy patches of hair and jagged teeth, didn't scare the brakeman as much as a derailment did. He waited until the creature was nearly on him again and rose to his knees, jabbing it in the stomach with his club. As it doubled over, hc swung and knocked the ghoul skidding over the far edge.

The thing was able to grab hold of the railing, but Archie had bought himself enough time to stagger across the car and jam his club back in the wheel. Looking frantically from the ghoul on the climb and the club, he gave it all of his remaining strength. Just as the grotesque creature reached him, the wheel broke free, throwing him backward into the ghoul, and then down between the cars.

From the gangway, Foley watched the ghoul fly from the top of the train and Archie's body fall under the wheels and then braced himself for the coming impact.

Cory was still reading quietly when Jess returned to the passenger car. He had convinced himself that she would never look on him with anything like affection and was therefore emboldened by a sense of simple civility. They'd spent the day together so he would ask for her name and perhaps offer to escort her from the train station in Phoenix to wherever she was headed next.

She smiled as he approached her seat, but then they heard the shouts of the men, and Jess was thrown off his feet by the lurching of the car as it left the tracks.

Foley followed his ghouls who jumped from the train as it neared the edge of the bridge and watched from the safety of the trees when the wheels hit the damaged tracks. The nose of the engine tipped into the expanse, splintering what remained of the ties as it crashed down to the creek below. The mail car swung wide, separating itself from the passenger car behind it and tunneling through the engine-sized hole in the bridge.

Cory's seat came unmoored from its base as the passenger car jumped the tracks. She reached for Jess, but he was tossed through a gaping split in the side of the car as it broke apart. Using her arms to shield her face from the shards of wood sailing through the air, she tumbled screaming as the car rolled down the ravine.

The livery and livestock cars telescoped into each other, grinding to a halt as their broken wheels tore up the ties. The surviving horses and goats burst through their demolished stalls and scattered in every direction. The caboose separated from the livery car and rolled onto its side when its wheels caught the damage in the tracks.

Jess cried out in confusion as he flew through the air, earth-sky-earth and then sky once more before finally the ground rushed up to meet him, hard and grating against his face.

The grim quiet that followed seemed even louder than the uproar of the crash. He heard only the whine of the wheels spinning on what was left of the overturned passenger car and the crackling of the flames as debris smoldered all around him.

Jess lifted his head, but it was so heavy that it fell back down and then there was nothing but blackness.

* * *

Fear closed around Cory's heart when she opened her eyes. It was not the damage, the fire, or even the memory of the crash that frightened her. She was terrified of the men running about.

Like the engineer, she'd assumed that the train was being robbed and though the bandits were probably close enough to hear, she couldn't help but cry out in pain while trying to hide herself. It was difficult to see her injury, but tears brimmed her eyelids because she knew that it was bad—very bad. Rolling onto her back, she reached for her side and then winced, pulling back her hand now covered in blood.

She turned her head away from the wound in frustration and then let out an astonished gasp at the sight of her luggage, not ten feet away. She bit down on her cheek to stifle her sobs and belly crawled the distance.

The pain in her side was nearly unbearable and her unsteady hands made searching through the bag almost impossible, but she was a woman who knew how to pack for a crisis and the striped shirt and felt hat she needed were near the top. While she'd never expected quite such a catastrophe, a train robbery *had* been high on her list of things that could go wrong.

If the robbers thought she was an injured man, maybe they would leave her to die out there in the middle of nowhere. Not ideal, but infinitely preferable to being dragged off, raped, and murdered by a gang of brutes. She replaced her red calico blouse, stripped off the skirt and petticoat, then wadded them up and threw them as far away from her as the light bundle would go.

She didn't think she could tuck the shirt into her pants without fainting from the pain, so the costume would have to do as it was, and she'd just found the perfect spot to play dead in the wreckage when a man's scream echoed through the ravine.

Cory recognized him as the conductor, only now he was being attacked. A tattered looking creature with gray, blotchy skin ripped open his shirt and bit down, tearing the flesh away from his neck.

Her main predator having always been the two-legged males of her own species, she hadn't given much thought to the dangerous animals that might live in the area and an old fear resurfaced. Bears. She'd never heard of bears in the desert but maybe, like everything else, they were quicker and more brutal out west.

She wasn't likely to be much help to him, but the man's screams would haunt her nightmares forever if she stayed hidden. After a quick scan of the wreckage, Cory made an adjustment to her survival strategy and reached for a twisted length of metal. The heat that radiated from it gave her pause and she reached underneath her shirt to tear away a piece of chemise. After wrapping the thin material around her hand like a bandage, she picked up the bar, wincing as the heat seeped through the barrier. Blistered palm or no, she could not turn back. With one hand she gripped it like a sword and with the other shielded her chest with the tapestry bag, then stumbled toward them.

When the conductor spotted her, he yelled, "Get away!"

His attacker turned toward her, and she then realized then that it wasn't a bear at all. Something in her had known all along that it was human, but she hadn't wanted to believe it. Now she had no choice. A strange and awful sort of human stared blankly at her with a chunk of flesh hanging from its teeth. Never taking its eyes off her, it wrapped its pale, gnarled hand around the weakened conductor's throat and choked him to death.

With his last breath, the conductor gurgled, "Get out...of here..."

Cory stood frozen in shock as the horrible thing proceeded to devour his torso. She could not run but, with her weapon and her bag clutched to her, she inched around to the side of the car and allowed herself one terrified sob before collapsing.

* * *

Face down in the dirt, Jess began to stir. Pain radiated throughout his entire body but after some experimentation it appeared that with enough effort, he could eventually get his extremities to move. Pressing himself up to all fours, he spit out a mouthful of blood and grit and then sat back on his heels.

His head swam as a not so small trickle of blood oozed from a gash in his temple. He gingerly touched his right eye, swollen and red from the impact of the rocks, and then scanned the horizon for the woman, but it wasn't the woman that he found.

A gruesome gray thing near the shattered passenger car appeared to be taking bites out of a dead man's body. Jess touched his eye again as if the injury was somehow responsible for the grisly scene, but instinct kicked in when the creature pulled off the dead man's arm. Jess felt for his pistol, drew, and fired.

The force of the bullet toppled the thing away from its victim, but rather than falling dead, it rose up and gave Jess a bloody-toothed sneer. He pulled back the hammer and fired again and again and though the thing eventually laid motionless, he was not at all convinced that he'd killed it.

Something poked at his side as he staggered to his feet, and Jess pulled his coat back for another surprise. The paper on Mark Chisolm's package had been damaged during his fall and the item hung precariously between his body and the pocket. He shook off the loose string to find himself holding an enormous hunting knife, sheathed in burnished leather and decorated with tribal markings similar to those he'd seen carved into rock formations all over Arizona. Markings even older than the tribes with whom his people were currently at war.

He slid the knife from its sheath and turned it over in his hands. The ten-inch blade, oddly serrated on both edges except at the point, protruded from a thick hilt wrapped tightly in strips of suede that matched the sheath in color. Jess had his own hunting knife, a priceless gift from Adam, but he guessed Mark's to be at least a century older and could understand why its safe delivery was worth so much to the mysterious man.

Even if he'd killed the thing he shot, Jess's curiosity wouldn't allow him to let it just lie there, but when he glanced up, it was gone.

Had he any peripheral vision on his right side, he could have reacted sooner, but at the sudden sound of fast footfalls he whirled around just in time to come nearly face to face with it. He swung the knife and slashed right across its middle as it leapt for him. *How had he managed such a meticulous slice?*

The thing gave him a sickly laugh and landed in a defensive crouch, shrugging off the cut and swiping at him with long claws as they circled each other. It moved on him quickly, but it wasn't very strong and, though his aching muscles screamed in protest, Jess lunged and took it to the ground.

As he straddled it, the creature scraped a claw across his head wound, blurring his vision once again. Fresh waves of pain vibrated down his back, and he could see little more than a dimming haze, but the blade grew heavy in his hands, guiding them forward to plunge the knife into the creature's chest. It gripped his forearms, shrieking out curses as Jess began to saw down the center of its body.

It writhed underneath him, howling in agony, but by the time the knife reached its belly the thing had stilled. Not satisfied, Jess stood up, took hold of its hair, and dragged the knife across its neck, relieved to learn that the blade was still sharp enough to sever the head quickly, and that whatever that creature was, it didn't bleed very much.

Jess doubled over with his hands on his knees, trying to catch his breath while scanning the area for more creatures. The only evidence of their numbers were random screams in the distance and his stomach turned over as he thought of the woman out there on her own.

Chapter Seven

He had to find her, but where to start? He sheathed Mark's knife and attached it to his belt, then took the bandana from his neck and tied it around his forehead, pressing it into the wound in a failed attempt to slow the bleeding. After surveying the damage to the train, he searched around the engine and worked his way back, hoping to gather supplies and survivors to help defend against whatever else might be lurking around. The afternoon sun was getting low over the mountains and the coming darkness would only add to their horrors.

Smoke still billowed from the stack, though much of it came from the nearby brush that caught fire when the engine crumpled at the bottom of the ravine. The mail car lay in pieces amidst a sea of kindled papers, their ashes floating upward, eerily veiling sections of the bridge that dangled over the destruction below it.

Jess carefully, and quietly, picked through the debris. Most of it was ruined or burning, but he did come across a lunch pail that contained a few pieces of dried meat, which he stuffed in his pockets.

Pausing near the distended corpse of the engineer, he unhappily determined that the face's awful contortions could not have been caused by the crash. He'd once seen a hanged man whose head was in better condition.

Jess spun in the direction of a sharp, high pitched whooping call coming from the swirling smoke. He thought it must have been an animal, perhaps something from the damaged livery car, but it wasn't a call he'd ever heard before. It repeated three times before the unnaturally thin man he'd seen leaning over the woman on the train came striding out of the wreckage.

Everything about him told Jess that the man was not merely a survivor of the crash. There was more to him, and it wasn't good. He crouched and peered around a pile of wood that had been thrown from the tender and then, from a safeish distance, followed the thin man back to what was left of the passenger car.

While he watched, Jess discovered that the man's nice clothes had been hiding even more peculiar features, and he was no longer completely sure that it was man at all. After draping his silk jacket over a detached axel, the thin man stooped over the conductor's body. Jess choked back a gag as he watched him use his skeletal hands to pull out the dead man's innards and weave them through his fingers, seemingly lost in thought. Then the thin man sniffed the air, wiped his hands on the dried grass and stalked around the car to where another body lay.

She'd seen him coming toward her through the smoke, his manner strangely threatening despite the gangly awkward way in which he moved. They'd never met, but she was certain that she knew him. The sense of dread he invoked was as familiar as the stench of mold and sulfur that overwhelmed Cory's senses as he neared. A dull pain stretched across her brow, emanating from where he'd touched her earlier, and as she rubbed at the spot it was as if a line of ants marched across her forehead. She pulled her hand away and fully expected more blood, but there was only grit on her fingertips. Cory laid as still as possible, hoping he would pass her by but somehow knowing that he wouldn't.

Foley took a knee beside her and ran a bony finger down her cheek. She was alone and afraid, but determination was the strongest scent she emanated, and that was one of his favorite seasonings.

He ignored the temptation to tear her apart, having sensed the bounty hunter on approach. If Foley let nature take its course, he had a feeling she would become the primary thread on which he could pull to manipulate his new prey.

Her head lolled back as he lifted her shoulders and a long mass of tangled curls tumbled out from underneath her hat. A strand of beads dangled from around his neck as he bent over her and, unable to fight her curiosity about the malformed man and mesmerized by how the spaces between the turquoise seemed to glow, she reached out for the necklace.

Foley smiled as she touched it, sensing that her powers of perception were uncommonly strong for her species. But he was smug in the knowledge that he'd warded the beads against every magical attack he could think of. The beads burned her fingertips, and he laughed when she recoiled with a yelp.

"You're not a very powerful witch, but I commend your efforts."

His awful face was only partially covered with skin so filmy she could see the hinges of his jaw when he spoke.

"It's a shame," he muttered, thinking to himself that if he didn't have to destroy her, she would make a fine apprentice. Oh, the things they could do...

Cory wasn't sure if he was still speaking to her or not as his gaze was all over the place, searching for something, or someone else.

Jess's pulse raced as he recognized the woman in the tall man's clutches. He noticed that she'd managed to change her clothes—probably thinking she would fool some bandits—and his already substantial respect for her soared; but there was no way she could have known what they would actually encounter that day.

He slid his fingers along the loops on his gun belt for extra ammunition and reloaded as he stumbled toward them, shouting, "Let her go!"

Unable to conceal his excitement, Foley let Cory's head fall and stood while rolling up his shirtsleeves to reveal long sinewy arms. He slid the brakeman's club from his belt and smacked the tip lightly in his empty palm. Half again as tall as Jess, who towered over most men, he stooped slightly, red eyes bulging out over his skeletal face to lock eyes with his target.

Foley could boast of striking terror into every human he had met since being banished to their Side of the veil, but Jess faced him squarely, standing as steadily as he could. With his good eye darting from the club to the woman, he kept his gun pointed at Foley's forehead, snarling, "Get back."

Grinning, Foley waved his arm and stepped aside to give him access to her. It was the extra row of sharpened teeth in his smile that finally pumped real fear into Jess's veins. He dropped to his knees, as much to protect her as that he no longer trusted his legs to hold him upright.

The letter from Mark Chisolm, the crash, the knife. Jess knew it was all connected, but he couldn't put it together. He had seen and touched these horrible creatures but did not dare trust his senses. What was real and what were the products of his distorted vision and the blood-soaked bandana around his head? And why did he feel so inexplicably drawn to this monstrosity of a man?

Jess pulled the woman close to him, looked up and asked, "What are you?"

"Take a good long look at me," he said, leaning down, "I am called Foley, and we will get to know each other well. Intimately well. We will meet again and again and again until one of us is dead." He arched a bony finger at Jess, "Hopefully you."

Sudden fury ripped through Jess. He would not allow man or beast or...Foley to taunt him like that. He hauled himself up and holstered his gun with twitching fingers hovering over the grip, ready to draw.

"I don't know why you're after me, but I would prefer to sort it out right now," he said, assuming that Foley couldn't be killed by a bullet any more than his thug could but hoping that like before, a decent shot could buy him some time.

He swayed on his feet, head swimming from the concussion and more certain by the second that he only had a few minutes to live whether Foley called him on his threat or not.

"I said, right now," he growled.

Foley threw back his head and laughed, shaking his

necklace until Jess caught sight of the fishhook tied to the strand.

"Yes, yes..." Foley clucked, "you are blood bound to me now—you are cursed as surely as I am."

"I don't understand," Jess staggered backward a bit. It was taking every bit of his strength to stay upright.

"You will, Jess Carson." Foley tipped his hat to Cory on the ground. "Ma'am."

Just then another of his ghouls rode over with Foley's silk jacket and an extra horse in tow. Buzzing flies circled the ghoul's head like a halo and Foley swatted them away in disgust as he swiped the jacket from its outstretched hand. He slipped it on and mounted his horse without further conversation, and as they galloped away, Jess sank to his knees again, shielding the woman from the dust and rocks kicked up by their departure.

When Jess rolled her away from him, the wide patch of blood on her shirt stuck to his coat. She panicked, pushing at his hands when he lifted the muslin to inspect her wound.

"No, please...no," she begged.

"You have to trust me," he took her by the chin and said, "I promise–look at me..." he gave her face a squeeze, forcing their eyes to meet. "I promise I only want to help you. Can you trust me?"

She did not trust him any more than she could trust that Foley creature. But she could not trust herself either because she now believed that she'd seen someone eaten alive by a monster. If he was true to his word, the man in front of her was likely the only chance she had for survival. If he wasn't, she supposed it wouldn't matter in the end, as close to death as she felt. Cory then remembered the sign on the train, "Proceed Here Safely", and gave him an almost imperceptible nod.

She squeezed her eyes closed when he shifted her undergarments and loosened her corset, biting her lip as he ripped away the fabric of her chemise to confirm that what he had feared was true. A roughly three-inch sliver of wood had wedged itself like an enormous splinter in her side.

"Dammit," he groaned.

Moved by his concern, but also realizing that there wasn't much he could do for her, especially given his own dire straits, she touched the fold of his bloody bandana and asked him, "Are we going to die out here?"

Jess had been wondering the same thing but hesitated at first to give her his honest opinion, mainly because he didn't want to hear himself say it out loud.

A not-so-distant bleating noise caught his attention then and for a moment he was afraid it was another one of those creatures, but a morbid laugh escaped his lips as something butted against him. They were in fact surrounded by creatures. Goats that escaped from the livestock car.

A heavier nudge at his shoulder nearly knocked him over and then a dirty tear ran from his blackened eye when he looked up to see Pepper staring down at them.

"Not gonna die today," he assured Cory, though tomorrow was another story altogether.

Jess dug his grateful fingers into Pepper's mane and tugged the horse down to their level before scooping the woman into his arms.

"My bag," she protested, reaching around him, "it's

everything I own."

He could certainly understand that and held her steady in the saddle while he strapped it to Pepper's side. He paused with one foot in the stirrup, unsure if he could make it up, but Pepper knelt again, and he swung his leg over just as the woman slumped unconscious against him.

A trickle of fresh blood escaped the bandana and his left eye had swollen completely shut.

"You've got to live," he whispered, to both of them.

Even Jess with his unreliable vision couldn't miss the little shack, swathed by the stars like some kind of desert lighthouse.

"Hello in there!"

He called out twice to no answer, so he made the awkward dismount with Cory in his arms and carried her to the door, which he found to be slightly ajar. After a sharp knock with his elbow, he pushed his way in.

"I don't mean any disrespect, but I've got an injured wom—" Jess stopped short.

Embers still smoldered red hot in the fireplace, but it was as if the owner had disappeared into thin air. Jess laid her down on a cot by the wall and lit a lantern, holding it out as he scanned the little one room house.

He noticed her shivering and covered her with his coat. There was an excessive chill in the cabin that didn't make sense, but Jess simply added that fact to the growing collection of oddities his mind had been collecting and moved to place another log on the fire. When reaching for the poker, an all too familiar sound put his entire body on alert, and he found the rattlesnake coiled between the iron rack and the wood box.

Using the poker, he fished the infuriated snake out of its warm hiding place and dropped it by the threshold where it stretched up, ready to strike. With a swing of the iron, he batted it outside and slammed the door just as the angry strike hit the wood with a thump. Jess leaned against the wall clutching the poker and breathing hard.

"Jesus," he gasped, before resuming a much more careful tour of the house.

A coffee pot sat on the mantle next to a tin plate and cup, and a cast-iron pot hung from a hook underneath. Next to the coffee pot was a clay urn nearly overflowing with disembodied rattle strings, evidently hacked off the ends of unluckier snakes. Jess plucked one out of the pot, gave it a little shake and put it back, thinking, *Adam would never believe this.*

Chapter Eight

A wooden trunk draped with a blanket served as a bench next to a table that was too large for the room but obviously a valuable workspace. It was cluttered with jars and bottles in various stages of full—full of what Jess could only imagine.

A water bucket and a pile of cleanish linen towels sat next to the table on the floor, reminding him of the unpleasant task at hand. Though he was grateful for the shelter, it gave Jess little comfort that the house had been so abruptly abandoned. Still, there was no point in borrowing trouble. He picked up the shotgun he found resting against the wall by the cot and, relieved to find it loaded, carried it outside, hollering out every now and then to make their presence known.

After tending to Pepper, he brought in their things, moved the jars aside and laid out supplies. Over the years Jess had cobbled together something of a medical kit which, in his line of work, had come in handy more than once. The kit would be inadequate for their needs that night, but he would make do, augmenting it with a flask of whiskey as necessary.

After searching through his possibles bag, he pulled out a small pouch containing a long needle and a spool of silk thread. The suture set had been a gift from a doctor friend who'd once stitched up his chin after a hostile fugitive clocked him with the handle of a whip. The hit hadn't broken his jaw, but the injury reduced him to a diet of nothing more substantial than mashed potatoes for several weeks. It was never Jess's first choice, but when the Marshal's order was for "dead or alive", he often found cause to opt for the former, and he slept alright, considering.

Unsure of how cooperative a patient she would be, he sat beside Cory on the cot and smoothed the hair away from her face, pleased that she wasn't feverish.

"Do you still trust me?" He asked.

When she nodded, he rolled up his sleeves, adding, "I'm afraid this is gonna hurt. Bad."

Smiling down at her clever disguise, he stripped off her muslin shirt, fully unlaced her corset and pushed away the rest of her layers. The offending piece of wood was buried crosswise but had inched out a bit during their ride, so he was able to work her skin around and extract the entire thing.

She braced herself for the burn and bit down hard on the inside of her cheek when he poured whiskey over the wound.

"There's no shame in cryin' out," he told her.

She was certain that if she allowed herself to cry, she would never ever stop so instead gave him an encouraging nod, hoping that he took the accompanying grimace as the smile it was intended to be.

Cursing his hazy vision, he stitched slowly. She kept quiet while he worked, gripping the side of the cot until her knuckles were white and she had no feeling left in her hands.

Dizzy, nauseous and trembling from the pain, she

forced her body to cooperate as he eased her forward to wrap a bandage around her middle.

"You would make an excellent seamstress," she croaked.

His reply was cut off as they were startled by a crashing noise at his back. Since there was no accompanying assault, he didn't bother to ask about it and she didn't bother trying to tell him that she'd just seen the coffee pot jump off the mantle.

"Rest now." He decided not to think about the noise and gave her a sip of water from his canteen before laying her back down. Moving to stoke the fire, his hands began to shake so badly that he could barely hold the poker, but he managed to take a long drink from his flask before situating himself on the trunk.

He leaned his back against the wall, watching the woman and going over in his mind the impossible events they'd endured since he freed her skirt from the nail. Her rest was fitful but that was to be expected, and he wondered at her resilience. And his own for that matter. Looking down, he noticed that his confidence had returned, or his sanity had left him altogether— either way his hands no longer shook.

The thing he killed was shaped like a man but...no...what could it have been? What could do such a thing and...why? Who is Foley? What's wrong with him and what did he mean by "intimately well"?

Just before he dropped off to sleep, Jess noticed that the coffee pot had fallen, and he could have sworn just then that he saw it skip across the floor as if someone had kicked it; but his eyelids were far too heavy for him to worry about it.

He woke to the sound of her wringing a linen towel into a basin full of water. She'd redressed in the bloodstained muslin shirt and arranged her hair into one long braid down her back.

He thought, *Adam would definitely never believe this.*

"I wonder why the owner of this cabin hasn't come back." Jess worried they wouldn't have time to explain their intrusion before said owner took understandable action against them.

Cory hung the towel over the bucket, unfolded an Indian blanket from the end of the cot and draped it over Jess's shoulders before taking a slow turn around the room. She stopped short at the fireplace as the vision of a man raving wildly at a sage bush pressed into the forefront of her mind. She shuddered as the man fell to his knees and then onto his side in a puff of dust.

"What's wrong?"

"Sometimes I'm a bit sensitive to my surroundings," she said in so near a whisper that Jess barely caught the words. "I don't think the owner of this house is ever coming back."

He tried to stand, but she laid a heavy hand on his shoulder.

"You're a mess."

After untying the bandana, she went to work with the wet towel, dabbing away the dried blood from his forehead. The cut wasn't very deep, but it had bled like an open vein.

She used her fingers to brush the dirt clumps from his thick hair, which was the same light brown color as his eyes. Cory gathered that he usually kept himself clean-cut, but that night his hair nearly touched his collar, and his goatee had grown out to a patchy beard.

She also got the impression that he was a dangerous man, she'd learned quickly that most of them out west were, but his injuries made him vulnerable, and his kindness gave her the courage to continue.

He winced when she went to work on his eye—first from the pain and then from embarrassment at the face she made when he did so. For a minute he thought he'd die from the shame, but he was so soothed by her touch that he was glad he didn't, and, painful or not, he could see much better when she was finished.

She rinsed the towel and gestured for him to remove his shirt, saying, "Fair is fair."

He chuckled at her matter-of-fact assessment of their predicament and then groaned as his body protested the movement.

Other than a few ugly bruises, his back and chest were reasonably free of fresh injuries, but she couldn't help noticing the obvious bullet hole scars as she cleaned him up.

"The horrors you've suffered..." she said, shaking the dust from the shirt.

He turned serious, bringing a hand to his chest. "You're assuming I didn't deserve this."

She'd so far survived a terrible ordeal that was apparently just beginning if Foley ended up being true to his word, and only because she'd put her trust in a man she knew nothing about. It could have been the sign on the train, a lapse in judgment brought on by exhaustion or simply the pull of those brown eyes, but something about him, whether he was good or bad, made her believe in him.

After a long minute, she handed him the shirt and said, "That's right."

Then she returned to the cot to rest. She was, frankly, surprised that in so many ways her strength held out for as long as it had.

Jess jerked awake a few hours later, this time finding her at the fireplace. Inasmuch as she could, she'd set the table and put the coffee pot to work. His stomach grumbled loudly at the sight of an orange and some biscuits.

"Oh no," he apologized, "I'm doing all the sleeping."

She reached for a pocket watch on the mantle that, having been busy rousting a rattlesnake, he hadn't noticed before.

"It's only just midnight." She replaced the watch, brought a cup of coffee to the table, and sat next to him on the trunk. "Our host appears to have been a solitary fellow, so we have to share. It's a bit strong—I took the liberty of adding some sugar, but I'm afraid there's no cream."

Jess breathed in the steam over the top of the cup. Adam always drank his coffee black and, as a young man, Jess wanted to be just like him but hated the bitter flavor until Adam convinced him to try it with sugar. It was a process, but he soon acquired the taste for it and even made notes in his book about which restaurants served the best cups.

"Here's my contribution." Jess retrieved the dried meat from his pocket and dropped it on the table, grateful she didn't ask about its origins.

They were starving but resisted the urge to devour everything like dogs after scraps and, instead, savored the simple meal as if it were high tea.

Since it appeared that they would be dependent upon each other for a while, she decided it was time to be honest with him and said, "You are Jess Carson."

He looked up from peeling the orange. "How do you know that?"

"I read a letter that fell from your pocket," she confessed.

"Where is it?" He stood up too quickly and had to hold his head as his vision blurred again. "Ow, dammit".

"I put it back." She tapped his chest where she'd returned the letter. "It was rude and presumptuous of me, but I wanted to know something about the man who saved my life."

He double-checked the letter and then sat down, pressing lightly on the bandage around his head.

"I believe we saved each other," he said handing her an orange segment and hoping she would forgive his overreaction.

She smiled and popped the orange in her mouth, quite pleased with his acknowledgement of her efforts.

"What do I call you?" He asked.

She folded her hands on the table, lifted her chin and said, "I have learned that you were once a wanted man, so it is only fair to tell you that you have been in the company of a divorced woman."

He furrowed his brow, "But you still have a name, right?"

She inhaled sharply before launching into her practiced explanation. Practiced only in her head as he was the first person other than a ticket agent to ask her name since she'd left her home some weeks earlier.

"My married name was Cory Elizabeth Boyle and

for a while I must continue to use Boyle for official matters, but I prefer Cory Elizabeth Lindsay, Lindsay being my father's last name. My real father that is."

"Miss Cory Elizabeth—"

"Actually, I've always found Elizabeth to be a bit pretentious."

"Miss Cory *Beth* Lindsay then," he suggested with a crooked grin.

"Cory will suffice."

Jess's eyes crossed. "Cory it is."

He leaned against the wall and stole a look at her out of the corner of his good eye. Cory was a smart, no-nonsense name and it suited her in that regard, but he would forever after think it was also the prettiest name he'd ever heard.

When panicking about the letter, he'd dislodged his bandage and now a dribble of blood escaped down his cheek.

"Hold still," she said, making some adjustments. When satisfied that it was secure, she began to pace the room, albeit a slow pace.

"I would read to you like a proper nurse, but I lost my book in the crash," she said with annoyance.

"Why don't you just talk to me then?"

"I don't know if I feel up to discussing those monsters just yet."

They were going to have to talk about it sooner or later, but he wasn't up for it either, so he asked, "Why did you leave him?"

Cory stopped in her tracks, and even Jess was a bit astonished by his direct question, but he didn't apologize for it.

She limped over to the basin and busied herself with

arranging the towel. "In point of fact he divorced me, but you can be certain that I am all the better for it."

He gestured to her injury and made a show of looking around the shack. "So it seems."

She gave him a smirk and continued, "My father died when I was nearly seven years old, but mother was far too beautiful to be a disregarded widow. Before my eighth birthday she had married Mr. Armstrong and provided him with my much-loved stepsister, Julia." She shook her head. "Another pretentious name but bless my mother—she had airs. Anyway, even though he was a cold man, Mr. Armstrong took care of us. I was attending Northwestern University when—"

"An educated woman? Is there no end to your scandalous behavior?"

Chapter Nine

Ignoring his commentary, Cory decided that under normal circumstances his sense of humor might be rather charming; but she was struggling to remember what normal circumstances were.

"When my mother died, Mr. Armstrong announced that he would rather I marry Angus Boyle than continue my education. Evidently, they knew each other during the war and," she shrugged her shoulders," some sort of deal was made."

Jess tightened his jaw thinking, *he sold her.*

"I rebelled at first," she explained, "but was then reminded of my position, which is to say that with my mother gone, I had no position, and I certainly didn't have the means to pay for university by myself. Angus instructed me to give him five sons," she shuddered, "but since he travels abroad most of the time, I believed that I could survive such an arrangement as long as I had the children to keep me busy."

Cory remembered Suzannah's pronouncement that husbands die all the time and her own daydreams about that very thing but decided not to share them with Jess.

"Did he keep your children?"

She hugged her arms around her body and looked at the floor. "He lost patience with me when it became obvious that I could not give him even one child, son or otherwise, let alone five."

Jess remembered how gently she tended his wounds and said, "I'm sure there's an orphanage somewhere in Chicago full of children who would give anything to have a mother like you."

"Angus Boyle? Adopt a child?" She was incredulous at the thought. "I suspect that, as it was, Mr. Armstrong had to call in a favor to get him to marry me since I am," she cleared her throat, "at twenty-seven, I was a bit older than some brides."

"Anyway, I'm thirty now and I've used my pitiful severance to come out west and make my own fortune."

He gave her that crooked smile again. "In the mines, I suppose."

"Near the mines."

He raised an eyebrow, his expression sobering.

"As a newspaper correspondent. I've heard," she lowered her voice as if telling a secret, "that mining towns are full of shocking stories."

"You heard right," he snorted, "did the tarot cards tell you that?"

"I read the cards for extra money but, truthfully, they don't say much." It was she who gave a rueful smile then. "There are other ways to find out what people need to hear."

"Like when you get...*sensitive?*"

Cory pressed a hand to her side and steadied herself against the table. "I couldn't see it all," she said, her face darkening with concern, "but something bad happened to the man who lives here."

He took her arm and led her to a seat on the cot. "We're both in need of a good nurse," he said, lifting her shirt to check the bandage over her stitches. He was pleased that the wound wasn't bleeding through, but she was obviously struggling to conceal her pain. He offered her his flask of whiskey, from which she allowed herself a hefty swig.

After taking another one himself, he asked, "Did you see anything when you touched my letter?"

She thought for a moment but as she opened her mouth to answer him the jars flew off the table as if someone had given them an arm sweep.

They'd been through so much that the commotion elicited scarcely a jump from either of them, but they did exchange exasperated looks.

Cory studied the smelly mess on the floor and pursed her lips. It had been years since her last spiritual encounter, but this was the second ghost she'd experienced in as many days. She wondered if possibly the noise in Chicago had blocked her access to such things and the vast wildness of the west made her more attuned to the supernatural.

Her mother would have warned that trouble was on the way, but trouble had already hit them—hard and fast. If she survived, it was more likely that her new life in Arizona was going to be complicated by her sensitivities and she would have to get serious, going beyond parlor tricks to keep her friends–she cast a glance at Jess—her only friend safe.

"My brother once said that burning sage will get rid of an evil spirit," he offered.

"There's no evil here." Cory rose and pushed at a piece of glass with the toe of her boot, remembering the sensation of Alain Auclair's hand around her neck. That was evil.

"Only anger and confusion."

"Do you think it's the owner of this cabin?"

She shrugged her shoulders. "All I know is that we're not alone here."

Just then the cast iron skillet dropped from its hook into the fire and the mantle began to shake until the plate and the pocket watch fell.

Jess led her to the fireplace and said, "Try again."

She stared hard into the fire but there was nothing except the sound of heavy breathing. She turned to give him an irritated look but behind him was playing out a vision of the owner of the cabin running for the door.

"He was panting, he ran outside...trying to get away from something."

Jess's eyes darted around the room. "Away from what?"

She shook her head, ignoring his question. "He fell by the water barrel next to..." Her eyes squeezed shut and then flew open. "Jess, he's next to the house."

"Shit." He grabbed the lantern and stumbled outside with Cory close on his heels. They had to duck around the back to keep from hitting their heads on the wrought iron tools hanging from the eaves over the rainwater barrel—and its owner.

"Poor, poor man," Cory whispered.

She looked up at Jess, who nodded and went back to find a shovel. On his way around the other side of the cabin he discovered a single horse stable where a buckskin mare peered out at him with suspicion from behind her wooden gate. He made a mental note to check on her later and then heard Cory scream.

He sprinted back to find that she'd turned the man over, upsetting two long diamondbacks that had been hiding underneath him. It was a cool night so they didn't act with the aggression of the one he evicted from in front of the fireplace earlier, but she stood frozen in place until he scooted them away with the shovel.

"Well," Jess put his arm around her shoulder, "at least we know what happened to him."

When her breathing finally slowed, he gave her a squeeze and dug the shovel into the ground. He'd slept a thousand nights under the stars and had never seen so many snakes in one place. It didn't make sense. Nothing made sense anymore. He knew there were plenty of monsters in the world, but it had always been his understanding that if a man left well enough alone, he could go his whole life without having to deal with one.

Confusion over their circumstances fueled resentment of his injuries, new and old. Exhausted and aching, he forced his arms into the correct position and stabbed the shovel down again. His right arm was unreliable and uncomfortable on the best of days, and this had not been one of those. As his frustration mounted, he stomped harder and harder on the shovel head, sweating and out of breath when he felt Cory's hand gently squeeze his arm.

"That will do," she said.

In the dark Cory hadn't noticed the sage bushes growing near the cabin, but as they piled rocks on the burial mound, the smell of death dissipated, and their heavy herbal scent was carried on the breeze. After plucking a handful of purple flowers to sprinkle over the grave, she crushed some leaves between her fingers and held them up for Jess to smell.

He wrinkled his nose in distaste but cut a bundle to take with them—just in case—before leading her to the stable.

"Oh, look at you," Cory cooed at the mare.

"I am apparently surrounded by beautiful females," Jess said under his breath.

She took the lantern from him and peered inside the well-kept stall, grateful that in the darkness, he could not see her blush. *You are not a schoolgirl*, she thought, and focused on the tack hanging from the walls.

Some odd-looking stitches fraying on a worn saddle blanket caught her attention and soon she realized that they were words, once part of some elaborate embroidery.

"Lov- lovely Priscilla," she made a face as she read out loud. "Good lord, is that your name? Priscilla?"

The horse pinned her ears back, remaining indifferent as Cory searched around outside the tiny stall, eventually finding a bucket of oats and then patiently waiting for Priscilla to acknowledge them in her outstretched hand.

"I didn't mean to hurt your feelings." Cory leaned a bit closer. "You *are* lovely and the name suits you very well."

"Do they teach city girls to ride these days?" Jess was teasing again but he wanted a serious answer. They would not abandon Priscilla, and their situation would be much improved if Cory were comfortable on horseback.

She put a hand on her hip and blinked at him. "Of course I know how to—"

Then a strange wind whipped around them, clanking the tools that hung from the eaves like violent wind chimes. Priscilla backed into her stall, and they had to cover their faces against the blowing dust that propelled them toward the front of the house. Jess noted with unease that the leaves on the bushes didn't move, and the wind only swirled around the two of them.

He glanced at the grave and said, "Someone's trying to get our attention again."

He handed her the shovel and drew his pistol, but as they burst through the door they were overcome once again by the stench of rot, and he realized sadly that his weapon would be of no use. One of Foley's ghouls squatted on the table with Jess's blood-soaked bandana hanging from its mouth.

Bile rose in his throat. The ghoul was shorter than the last one and must have once been a boy no older than twelve or thirteen.

The young thing held a torch made from one of the linen towels wrapped around the tip of the fireplace poker. The bandana fell from its mouth as it began to laugh and dance atop the table, reaching up to light the ceiling on fire. The dry and splintered wooden beams caught instantly but before the ghoul could hop down, Cory swung the shovel and smacked it off the table.

As the ghoul hit the floor the flame from the torch caught the Indian blanket and engulfed the cot. The creature moved to grab the iron poker, but Cory brought the shovel down over and over on its head until Jess took it from her.

"Get our things," he ordered.

While stuffing their belongings into their bags, Cory felt something on the toe of her boot and then teetered, woozy with fear as two rattlesnakes slithered from underneath the cot, over the belly of the ghoul and out the door.

Jess shook his head but there was no time to ponder

the *what ifs*. Cory had incapacitated the ghoul for sure, but he steadied himself for what had to be done next. Looking away from the young face, he stomped down hard on the step of the shovel, slicing through the ghoul's neck with the blade.

She could hear its grisly death over the crackle of the flames but hoisted the shotgun with their bags and kept her eyes on Jess, crouching to stay below the smoke as they staggered out of the cabin.

They piled their bags outside next to Pepper and then ran to the stable. Priscilla bucked as they led her out, but she was convinced, grudgingly, by the encroaching flames to be saddled.

Once their belongings were secured, Jess gave Cory a boost and hollered, "Let's get the hell away from here!"

Cory held tight to the reins as Priscilla reared up. It was not ideal, and maybe not even possible, but she would have to earn the horse's respect during the ride. She leaned close to her ears and spoke sweetly but urgently as she patted her neck. Priscilla turned around, cantered a bit and then took off, more anxious to get away than to obey Cory's commands.

Once the cabin was a distant inferno, Cory said, "Whoa...whoa," pulling gently on the reins. When Priscilla ignored her, she gave a sharp tug. "I said, whoa."

Priscilla tossed her head around but did as she was told, albeit with a show of indignant stomping that made Cory's dismount far less graceful than it might have been.

To hide his laugh, Jess gazed out at the thin orange line on the horizon. His head was throbbing, he was exhausted and starving, but the sight of the sunrise behind his brave hearted companion gave him an absurd amount of comfort.

She dug around in her bag, then lifted her shirt and wrapped the corset around her middle, reaching behind her back to pull the laces tight.

"I don't want my good doctor's stitches to come loose," she explained with a smile.

He swung down from Pepper, found his canteen and took a long swig of water. "Christ woman," he said, handing it to her, "you are a fearless thing."

Her smile widened, hiding her relief at his incorrect assessment. She was living the thrilling life that she specifically came out west to find—and she was absolutely terrified.

Chapter Ten

Two scrawny young coyotes raised their hackles when Mark led his horse through the carnage of the train crash. The coyotes at first could not believe their luck after spotting nine goats, some of them wounded, roaming so close to their den; but these men were an unwelcome interruption intent on scattering the herd.

Augie clapped his hands at the coyotes, snapping, "Go on now!"

Reluctant to give up their fortune, the coyotes stood their ground, snarling at Augie until he cocked his lever action rifle and fired it over their heads. It would not do for a coyote, even in the middle of nowhere, to get the idea that it was okay to attack livestock, and he gave Mark a satisfied nod as they ran off.

Mark Chisolm and the Reverend August Ortega picked their way through the bodies until they came upon the ghoul Jess had beheaded. Mark smiled to himself. As he'd hoped, Carson was quick on the uptake, and thankfully neither he nor the Lindsay woman were among the dead. Only one set of horse tracks led away from the ravine so he figured that they must have ridden away together. It was difficult to tell how much of the blood soaked into the ground was theirs, and he could only hope their injuries hadn't turned out to be fatal.

Augie picked up the ghoul's head by the hair and flung it as far away from them as his sixty-year-old shoulder would allow. The Southern Pacific clean-up crew would be in for a surprise when they found it—and they would, since not even the coyotes were likely to go near the foul thing.

"Think they made it all the way to Black Canyon City?" He asked.

"No," Mark said, "but they would have made it to Burl Westin's place by now. He's only about four miles from here."

Augie grunted in agreement. Westin was an odd loner known for his obsession with rattlesnakes. The story was that he'd been bitten by a Diamondback as a youngster and left a tad touched by the experience. He'd never forgiven the audacity of that serpent and developed a lifelong revenge fantasy involving all reptiles. Unnerving as he was to be around, the locals swore by Burl's antivenom, and it was rumored to be an effective treatment against the bites of any number of slithering things.

Mark crouched over the ghoul, took a stick and poked around in its chest cavity, conveniently vented by Carson, until he located the heart. Even a talented necromancer like Foley would find it difficult to reanimate one with no head, but that didn't mean he wouldn't try. Thick black blood bubbled out of the ghoul's heart as Mark stabbed into the shell of its corpse. *Dead. Forever this time.*

Augie took a knee beside him and said, "If there are any more, they went with their master."

"You know there are more."

Mark rose, put his hands on his hips and turned in

a slow circle. The early sunrise and the glow of the remaining little fires gave the scene a hellish backdrop scored by the yipping of the stubborn coyotes.

Though raised by his father's people, Mark Chisolm had the look of his mother. Tall, with thick black hair, only recently graying around his temples. His emerald eyes were accentuated by sharply lined features that appeared fair enough for his presence to be unquestioned almost anywhere he went. Even so, he had learned over the years that hiding his face and keeping to the shadows served his purposes even better.

"They'll be moving slow," he told Augie as he mounted his horse, "so go and wait for them in Black Canyon City."

Augie gestured toward what was left of the Conductor. "We can't just leave the dead like this."

"Like what?"

Impossible man, Augie thought, then took in a sharp breath and pointed to a fire in the distance.

"Shit," Mark said, following his gaze.

"I guess they just can't catch a break," Augie mounted his own horse, but Mark stopped him from racing toward the fire.

"Foley has made Carson a target," he said, thinking out loud, "and that's good."

"Good?"

Mark thought for another minute and added, "Get them to lure Foley into town."

"Black Canyon City?" Augie was aghast.

"No, our town."

"He would never go back there."

Mark stared at the mutilated ghoul and pictured Carson and the woman, wounded but determined to survive.

"He won't be able to help himself."

* * *

"God dammit," Jess swore as the cut over his eye began leaking through the bandage.

Priscilla reared up slightly, annoyed by the way Cory's weight was distributed compared to her former rider.

"We're stuck together, so you needn't be so fractious," she scolded.

Jess sniffed. "Are you talking to me or the horse?"

"I suppose after all that's happened, this whole party is eligible for some petulant behavior, but I'm not cross with you."

"Hmph," he grumbled, "give it time."

Priscilla allowed her to slow, and she said, "Let me redress that bandage for you."

He shook his head. "We're not far from Black Canyon City."

They rode in silence until Cory tired of his dour mood. She recalled seeing another name on his letter from Mark Chisolm and asked, "Who is Adam Colter?"

At this, Jess couldn't help but smile. "Adam is my brother."

"His surname is Colter. Are you half-brothers?"

"We have different fathers," he admitted, "and different mothers too."

He laughed at Cory's obvious confusion and then explained to her how Adam had found him as a teenager, and how his arm was broken, and how there was no one in the world he trusted more.

She hesitated for a bit over the obvious question, but he seemed so comfortable talking about the man that she dared to ask him, "Why were you wanted men?"

Jess didn't answer her at first, he only rubbed subconsciously at his chest until she regretted asking.

"Don't trouble yourself with the memory, Jess. I shouldn't have—"

"Adam's woman tried to rob a bank," he said, barely able to control the anger in his voice, "and I tried to stop her, but everything went wrong, and a man died."

"They blamed the two of you," she surmised.

He nodded. "I'd been shot, and Adam took a huge risk by delivering me to some friends of ours, but then he had to go on the run."

"He sounds like a good man."

Jess laughed out loud. "He is not; nor is he my blood, but he's my only family. I was searching for him when..." he gestured vaguely in the direction of the train crash, "but I'll never stop looking."

Cory had no doubt of that. She remembered how clearly she'd seen Adam's face in her dream and because of that felt a strange closeness to them both. It went beyond what she and Jess had already been through together. For confirmation, she asked, "Does he have dark hair?"

Jess turned abruptly in the saddle to face her. "Did you see him when you touched my letter?"

She explained that her visions weren't usually triggered by touch and that she had seen the two of them in her dream on the train. When he pressed, she admitted that there wasn't much more to tell, and she'd been so rattled by her experiences with the Auclairs that she wasn't completely sure of anything that happened right before the crash.

He coaxed the story of Yvonne's ghost out of her and at first thought, *that explains the bruises and the torn dress.* Then he set his jaw, vowing silently that if they ever met, he would save Suzannah the trouble by killing Alain Auclair himself.

"It must have been Mark Chisolm who showed up to help, but what does he want with you?"

She shrugged. "We're all connected somehow, but I swear I'd never met the man before then."

Cory was afraid to tell Jess about the warning Adam gave her in the dream, but the more they learned about one another, the more she was afraid of what might happen if she didn't.

"Adam rides an Appaloosa?"

Jess blinked at her. "Alice the Second."

"I believe the two of you were looking for a fishing spot...you held a pole."

"Adam didn't have the patience for fishing, but he'd humor me now and again." Jess attempted to wink at her, but it was more of a blood encrusted twitch. "Especially if we were hungry enough."

She repeated Adam's warning, and though it would not have surprised either one of them to learn that the Devil *was* listening in, they couldn't figure out the link to Mark Chisolm. Neither one was ready to question how Foley played into it all.

"I wouldn't have thought it possible, but we know even less now than we did before."

She hated to have disappointed him so, and he'd grown tired of talking again, but she had one more, rather burning question for him.

"Alice the...second?"

Jess laughed. "Alice the first died of old age. She was also an Appaloosa—sweetest animal you'd ever meet—he was truly broken hearted, but Alice the Second is good natured enough. I assume they're still together. Somewhere."

He then drew her attention to the tiny town at the top of the hill. "Black Canyon City."

She smoothed the hair away from her face. "We look a mess."

"They don't judge where we're going. They don't dare."

* * *

"Lordy be!" Ada Wheeler hobbled around the counter as fast as her crutch would move her. "Jess Carson, what have you done to yourself?"

She looked Cory up and down. "And where did you get this grubby little thing?"

Cory bristled at that, but then figured the woman was probably being kind with the word grubby.

"The train derailed," she stammered, "and we—"

"You were on that train?" Cole Wheeler had been stocking canned peaches on a shelf high above the counter. Jess tensed, hoping the older man didn't fall as he descended from an unstable ladder to greet them. "Half the men in town rode out there to help clean up the mess. You're lucky to be alive."

Cole stuck out a calloused hand and Jess gave it a rough shake, nodding in Cory's direction. "This is Cory Lindsay, and we've had one hell of a long night. I was hoping..."

"Of course, good gracious! Cole let's take them next door."

In their younger days, Ada set her sights on Cole Wheeler when he first opened the general store in Black Canyon City. Her romantic hopes were dashed when a bout of scarlet fever left her severely weakened and arthritic at the age of eighteen. However, the twenty-five-year-old Cole was so smitten with Ada that he proposed at her bedside. They argued constantly, but she would tell anyone who'd listen that his love saved her life back then. There were no children but together they operated the general store until she inherited the hotel next to it from her father, making them the town's most successful family of two.

Cole gave Jess a sideways look. "Have you got any money?"

"You greedy old thing!" Ada chided over her shoulder, already leading Cory to the door.

"I can pay for the trouble," Jess assured him.

"No trouble at all." Ada adjusted her crutch and wrapped her arm around an exhausted Cory, who found it almost impossible to climb the stairs. "We help each other around here."

After Cole poured a final bucket of hot water in the tub, Ada scooped in the Epsom salts and shooed him out of the room so Cory could take off her clothes.

"Good gracious!"

Cory twisted around in vain, so Ada led her to a full-length mirror where she finally got a look at her stitches.

"I imagine that's Mr. Carson's handiwork."

Cory nodded. The stitches were neat, but the wound

was red and ugly. Tears brimmed her eyelids and she had to turn away from her haggard reflection. "I suppose I'm lucky that we found each other," she choked out before stepping into the tub.

The warm water rose all the way to her underarms, and it was not only the first comfort she'd had in days, but it felt so good that Cory rested her head on her knees and lost what little hold she still had on her emotions.

Ada felt for the younger woman but wasn't keen to let her sit there so pitiable with her entire body shaking with sobs. She plopped down on the bed and asked, "Where do you come from?"

"Chicago," Cory sniffled.

Ada let out a long breath. "Life couldn't have been easy for you in the city, or you surely wouldn't have come out here—"

"I'm not going back." Cory wiped her eyes and reached for the soap.

"Then pull yourself together, girl." Ada's once kind voice was now tempered with a harsh warning, "This is the west. It's all hard livin'—hard dyin' too, even if you're careful."

"I'm not going back," Cory repeated, scrubbing her arms, amazed at how much grime came away with each swipe of the washcloth.

Ada laid a dressing gown over the chair and said, "I better go make sure Cole hasn't drowned that poor man."

"How do you know Jess?" Cory asked.

"He passed through town a while back, lookin' for his brother," she started, "and huntin' for a murderer."

Cory squeezed out the washcloth and then paused

before unbraiding her hair. "He found the murderer, didn't he?"

"That he did." Ada gave her a thin-lipped nod and left the room.

When the water went cold, Cory slipped on the dressing gown and went to the window. Jess was out back, in fresh clothes and a cleaned-up goatee. He sat on a fence rail, writing in his book.

Probably listing the instructions for relieving a cannibalistic man beast of his head, she laughed to herself and then grimaced.

"Put it over there," Ada ordered Cole to deliver a tray of food and when he left, she drew Cory away from the open window. "You'll catch your death, girl."

Cory followed her nose to the tray loaded with fried chicken, biscuits, gravy and what appeared to be apple cobbler.

"Cole made the biscuits, so I soaked them in gravy. You don't want to break a tooth."

Cory was already gnawing on one, so grateful that her eyes reddened again. Ada moved to close the window and said, "Oh, I see what you were lookin' at," as she noticed Jess in the yard.

"I beg your pardon?" Cory found it difficult to be indignant while mumbling with her mouth full.

"He's a fine specimen, but surely you know by now that Jess Carson is an unsettled man."

"I've been settled," Cory said, spooning up some cobbler, "and I'm beginning to think that his way might be better."

"I suspected as much," Ada sighed, "so I brought you this." She held out the most unusual piece of clothing Cory had ever seen.

"What in the world?"

"It's called a split skirt," Ada explained. "It's not as vulgar," she gave Cory's pants a sideways glance, "and there'll be less chafing if you insist on riding that obnoxious horse."

Cory swallowed another bite of rock-hard biscuit and gave it a second to travel down her throat before she said, "How can I ever thank you, Mrs. Wheeler."

Ada held up Cory's stained and torn clothes. "You can let me burn these pants."

Chapter Eleven

"You look a hell of a lot better than you did when you got here." At Ada's instruction, Cole had brought another tray of food out for Jess. He moved in close to inspect the damage to Jess's eye. "The swelling's already going down."

Indeed, Jess could see much better. His gaze travelled to the house, but the windows were closed. "How's Cory?"

"You won't catch me tryin' to assess a woman's condition. Besides, I haven't seen much of her since Ada whisked her away."

"The horse she's riding belonged to someone who lived outside of town. I was hoping you could tell me about him."

"Lived?"

"We found him snake bit on the side of his shack," Jess explained. He told Cole how they buried him and how the place had burned down, leaving out the part about the man's ghost and the ghoul's role in the fire.

"Burl Westin." Cole hung his head. "Rest his soul. It was bound to happen, the way he lived alone out there with all those reptiles. Say, you didn't happen to bring any of his famous anti-venom with you?"

Jess shook his head, remembering the jars on the table and wishing he'd known what they were at the time.

"Westin wouldn't let me sell the anti-venom in the store, he said people could come visit if they wanted it that bad, but hardly anyone would dare go out to that place."

"Did he have family in town? His horse…"

"Even if he did, they wouldn't want Priscilla. Damned irritable beast. Your friend can have that horse, if they can stand each other."

Jess's full belly seemed to weigh down the rest of him and his steps were so heavy that he had to take a break on the way to his room, leaning against the hallway just inside the hotel. Still, he paused for a few moments outside Cory's door with his hand raised to knock. Hearing no movement inside he thought better of it and moved on down the hall. His head swam so with fatigue that he doubted he could form sensible words anyway.

He paced around his room for a while, then took inventory of every single thing he had with him. Thankfully, not much had been lost and he would shop the Wheeler's store in the morning to replenish the few things they would need on the road to Phoenix.

It occurred to him then that Cory might not want to travel with him anymore, not that he could blame her, but with that thought came an unexpected jolt of sadness. He ignored it and chided himself for being ridiculous, but then anxiety set in. Foley had made it clear that for whatever reason, he would be back for them. Both of them. And though he doubted she enjoyed his companionship as much as he enjoyed hers, it wasn't safe for them to split up.

She's a pretty...pretty clever woman, he thought to himself, hoping that she would understand the danger, hoping she would want to stay with him.

Spinning the cylinder on his pistol, he reloaded and carefully packed up his things before making sure Mark Chisolm's letter was tucked into his breast pocket and then finally taking off his boots. A quick check under the bed would become a lifelong habit after watching those rattlers slither out from underneath Burl Westin's cot.

He flopped on top of the covers and put his hands behind his head with plans to lay there and figure out how Foley was connected to Mark and how they were all connected to Cory Lindsay, but he was sound asleep before he could think about anything at all.

Jess found Cory the next morning dropping a coin into a guitar player's case on the steps of the general store, just as Cole came out with a broom to shoo the musician away.

"Leave him alone!" Ada hollered from inside, "this place could use a little culture."

Cole gave Jess an exasperated look and said, "Culture, but not talent, I guess."

Unwilling to enter that particular argument, Jess shrugged and gave Cory his arm. They could not compare to the grand department stores in Chicago, but she had learned to think of each little shop out west as an oasis. All carried some oddity, new to her, that she'd never imagined would become necessary for survival or, she smoothed her split skirt, ease of survival.

She'd been unwilling to let Ada burn her pants and

when she explained her reason for the costume, the older woman relented but convinced her to buy a new pair.

The Wheeler's store carried the usual bolts of fabric and kegs full of nails, shot and candy, as well as salt, sugar, tobacco, and medicine. Cory was amazed at the supply of ready-made goods. Since their final stop would be Phoenix, just over a day's ride, Jess and Cory needed only a few basic supplies. Even so, they took advantage of the variety and filled a basket between them.

"Look at that," Cory said, drawn to a single shelf lined with books. Jess reached around her and selected one titled *Moby Dick*.

"Have you read this?" He asked Cole.

"Ha!" Ada snorted, "Never in life. But if *you're* a reader, Miss Lindsay, I have a recommendation." She pumped her eyebrows at Cory and handed over a copy of *Madame Bovary*. "Read it now before it gets banned."

"Banned?" Cory held it to her chest as if someone were already trying to take it from her. "Is it so audacious?"

"I suspect you can handle it," Ada said with a wink.

"Are we doin' business or what?" Cole made a show of taking out his ledger book. "In addition to one night's room and board, you've got here two boxes of ammo, *Moby Dick*," he sniffed and rolled his eyes, "one blue bandana, one man's shirt, a tin of coffee, some dried beef, dried strawberries—say, don't you want these peaches too?"

Jess nodded. "Sure, why not?"

Cole put the peaches in the pile and continued, "six hard candies and two pencils," he said, carefully writing up Jess's receipt. "You want those pencils sharpened?"

Jess gave him a strange look and said, "I have a knife."

"Wait 'till you see this." Cole could not keep the excitement out of his voice as he led him to a device mounted at the end of the counter, stuck the pencil in and turned the handle.

"I'll be damned." Jess shook his head in disbelief.

"You try it," Cole insisted.

Cory exchanged perplexed looks with Ada as the men marveled over the new technology.

Ada grumbled, "Look at all that mess it leaves on the floor," and went back to work in the storage room.

Cory interrupted their sharpening and piled her purchases on the counter: a small bag of dried apples, a jar of pickles, a new straw riding hat to replace the one she'd lost after the crash, a tin coffee cup and a pair of pants. She eyed the other men's clothing with longing— it was so much more comfortable—but had taken Mrs. Wheeler's advice to heart. She wanted to fit in and reluctantly selected a woman's button-down blouse.

Cole turned and hollered, "How much for all these clothes?"

"No charge for the clothes!"

"What?"

"Mrs. Wheeler, that's very kind but—"

Ada lumbered back out to the front of the store and cut off Cory's protest. "We don't charge people what we had to clothe from nothin'," she snapped at her husband, "the child came in here wearin' pants for goodness sakes. Pants!"

"Well, I don't count the hat," Cole grumbled.

Cory looked back and forth nervously between the

two of them. "Of course not."

"Don't forget to tell them about the message," Ada shouted.

Jess was ecstatic. "A message from Adam? Is it?" He stretched over the counter, but Cole held the paper just out of his reach.

"Telegram for Miss Cory Lindsay," he said.

Cory gave Jess a guilty shrug, "I don't know who it could be from, I didn't even know that I was going to be here."

Such news. Have learned a practical skill. Will tell all in Phoenix. Much love. Suzannah.

"Good lord, she might have killed him already." Cory handed the telegram to Jess, who curled his lip at the news.

"Good riddance," he sneered, "you're sure there's nothing for me?"

Cole shook his head and then said, "Sign here for the telegram, Miss," adding, "Ada, come see! We got a southpaw in the place." He tut tutted in her direction. "It's not natural, you know. Not very ladylike neither."

"Well, I assure you, I don't do it on purpose," Cory snipped.

She opened her purse, but Jess nearly knocked them both over to get in front of her, signing his name to both receipts.

"Two lefties at the same time have got to be bad luck," Cole mumbled.

Jess grinned at Cory and said, "You have no idea."

"How much for everything, including the books."

Cole rang up the charges on the big brass till. "That'll be...five dollars and fifty cents."

"Jess!"

"Calm down," he thumbed to the restaurant across the street, "you're buying us breakfast."

* * *

Cory gave a little curtsy as Jess held the door open for her at the restaurant. Her eyes flashed as she brushed by and quietly informed him that she would pick up the heaviest item she could swing and blacken *both* of his eyes if he ever told her to calm down again.

There were flecks of violet in Cory's blue eyes that danced when she was angry and also when she laughed, which to Jess's relief was more often, at least when no one was trying to kill them.

In no time, they were digging into plates of eggs and bacon that did not come with gravy but included one, considerably softer, biscuit each.

He'd also ordered a bowl of oatmeal that Cory eyed suspiciously. The only oatmeal she'd ever eaten was clumpy, bland and full of raisins, but he'd become quite a connoisseur after getting his jaw whipped and he'd decided that Black Canyon City served up the very best.

"You have to try it," he insisted, holding out a spoonful. "Canned peaches are a big thing around here, they put them in everything."

She reluctantly let him feed it to her and then picked up her own spoon.

"May I?" She asked, already digging in.

Her eyes rolled back in her head as she savored the peaches, brown sugar and cream. She'd not had anything so rich and sweet in ages.

Before the oatmeal arrived, Cory had been

describing for him a restaurant in Chicago, and in the middle of the story she caught him smiling to himself.

"Are you laughing at me?"

"Absolutely not," he assured her, "but you seem happier saddled on a horse—Priscilla no less—than you would be saddled with some giant overbearing asshole of a husband, no matter how rich and handsome he is."

"He's no giant," she laughed, "and, certainly not handsome. Not like you anyway. His features are more..." she cocked her head, "delicate. But you're right, he is a rich, overbearing asshole."

Jess blushed bright red. "The things you say woman, and the things you do. This part of the country is tough, but here you are, braving it all like some kind of storybook adventure goddess."

"Your mother must have been even braver to raise a family in these parts when she did. Did your father mock her too or—"

"I suspect she was dragged out here kicking and screaming." Jess gave her a sad smile, but that's according to my grandpa. My folks died when I was a little boy, so I don't remember much about them."

"I'm sorry, you must have missed them so."

He waved off her concern. "You can't miss what you never knew you had."

As if reading his mind, she said, "Have you any idea at all where Adam might be?"

He drew in a deep breath and let it out slow. "My leads had run dry, and then I got this letter. He patted his chest to make sure it was still there. "I think Mark Chisolm must know something, but I've got to find him first."

Jess slid his hand to where he now wore Mark's

knife strapped to his leg, no longer concerned about the attention he might draw because of its size. Given what he knew about those man eaters, easy access was everything.

They shared the rest of the oatmeal in silence and finally, she said, "Are we going to talk about that...that strange man? The one from the train?"

He'd put it off for as long as he could, as if not mentioning it somehow meant that none of it had really happened. But it did—all of it. In only a couple of days, he'd been acquitted of his *crimes*, his train had crashed, he'd killed flesh eating monsters, he'd been cursed by a madman, and—he eyed her over his coffee cup—he'd made a traveling companion out of a smart, pretty, kindhearted woman. He'd read books that were less exciting only his story was really happening, and though the excitement was getting old fast, he feared it was just beginning.

After another sip of coffee he said, "I don't think Foley's a man. And those creatures, they aren't men either. Not anymore. I've seen all kinds of strange things out here and I've heard of even more, but I always thought that ghouls were just sick people dying from something they didn't have a name for. Until now, that is."

From the next table, Augie's ears perked up. He shared an expectant glance with his companion, an enormous, sunbaked, leathery man dressed in a gray sarape that, stretched across his broad shoulders, made him look even larger. The man said nothing but leaned his chair back slightly to hear everything the soft-spoken woman had to say.

"Ghouls," Cory repeated, searching her memory for

scary stories from her childhood. "They're raised from the dead. Do you think Foley made them?"

"That takes magic. Powerful, dark and ugly magic."

"He crashed the train, didn't he?" The more she thought about it, the more her fear of Foley turned to hatred.

Augie gave his companion a knowing look and leaned forward on his elbows.

Jess's narrowed his eyes and shoved back his chair. "I think we're about to find out." He opened his coat, laid a hand on the grip of his pistol and rose to tower over the table next to them.

Chapter Twelve

"Relax," Augie held up his hands. "I'm a friend."

Jess kicked away the extra chair in front of him. "Do you want to tell me why you're so interested in my conversation, *friend*?"

He'd only just finished his question when the large man in the sarape had him shoved against the wall. Jess's face contorted with pain, but he could tell that the giant hadn't used a fraction of the force he could have and that confused him even more. He was tired of being confused. He stomped on the top of his attacker's foot, but only elicited a growl of annoyance.

"Good lord!" Cory jumped up and latched onto the big man's bicep, pulling with all her weight. "Let him go!"

Both men looked down at her and then back at each other. The big man snorted with laughter, and Jess rolled his eyes and then Augie stepped around to her side.

"We don't mean any harm, ma'am."

He slapped his friend on the back and said, "It's okay," and when Jess had been released, Augie leaned close to his ear and whispered, "Mark Chisolm sent me."

The chatter in the restaurant had long since quieted and all eyes were on them.

"Let's go somewhere we can talk."

"I hope you're planning to pay your bill first." The restaurant owner tapped a thick baton on the tabletop.

Cory smiled sweetly. "Of course we are."

When she stooped to right the chair, Jess handed him twice the cost of their breakfast to cover the scene they'd caused. It had been her intention to add a little more to the bill as well but when she realized that Jess paid it, she stomped along behind the men, fuming. Outside, Jess gave her a look that said he knew why she was mad and that he didn't care.

In the alley between the restaurant and the saloon, Augie said, "I'm the reverend August Ortega, but most people just call me Augie."

Augie's friend looked around to make sure they hadn't been followed, and Jess instinctively did the same, wondering who or what the big man was searching for.

"Since when do preachers need protection?" He asked, nodding at his companion.

"Oh, you'd be surprised." Augie said, "Eduardo looks after me when I'm on the road."

"Where is Mark Chisolm?" Jess started, "How does he know me?" He pulled the knife from its sheath and held it up. "Where in the hell did he get this? What does Foley want with me and...what *is* Foley?"

Augie said, "I can tell you that Mark knew you'd be needing that blade," he lowered Jess's knife hand, "but you don't need it right now."

"Where is he?"

Augie looked to the sky. "I don't ask questions I don't want the answer to."

Jess said, "Well, I do," but he was beginning to think

that his new acquaintance might have the right idea.

"Fine," Augie sighed, "Mark will tell you everything you want to know, and we'll help you find him."

"Now?"

"Now, and if we leave this minute, we'll be in Phoenix by tomorrow afternoon."

Jess felt Cory's hand on his forearm and said, "I'll need five minutes."

He didn't dare assume that she wanted to travel any farther with him and she certainly didn't deserve to be burdened with his dangerous troubles.

"The Wheelers will help you arrange some safer travel," he told her.

Panic rose in Cory's chest as she sensed that she was about to be abandoned again. It was true that Jess Carson was cursed, but most people thought she was too. An unconventional woman cursed by her odd sensitivities and rendered useless by her so-called barren womb.

Jess came with danger, but evidently so did everything else out west, so she put her hands on her hips and tried to keep the quiver out of her voice. "You said yourself that this is harsh land, so we should stay together—form some kind of partnership until our probable untimely passing."

Jess turned away from her; afraid that the joy would show on his face. Then he more sternly turned back, ashamed of himself for wishing Cory to join him on such a deadly path.

"You'll be safer on your own."

Safer on my own? She thought, *ha.* "Even if that were true," she argued, "I wouldn't leave you to face this devilry alone and when it's all over, I'll help you find your brother. Assuming we survive."

"I thought you wanted to write about scandalous mining towns."

"Don't you think our story is more interesting than some mining town?"

She'd obviously never been to Oatman, Arizona, but he said, "Interesting is not the word I would use."

They locked eyes for a long moment and then each nodded in an unspoken agreement. It might as well have been a blood oath as far as Cory was concerned, but Jess intended to be more flexible if she wanted out. Part of him wished that she would, but his anxiety for her safety was tempered by the fact that he was ridiculously happy to have her along. He hated himself a little bit for that.

He led her to Priscilla and prepared to give her a boost, but she drew a ragged breath, set her jaw and said, "I can do this."

* * *

Since they'd left Prescott, the pine trees had given way to cedars, and then to saguaros. The air warmed considerably but thankfully they were shaded by mesquites and sycamores as they traveled south along the Agua Fria River.

While they set up camp, Eduardo, who'd barely said a word up to that point, chuckled to himself as Augie took the opportunity to try saving some souls.

Jess sniffed in annoyance when the preacher opened his Bible and said, "Unfortunately, I've killed a few men, Augie."

"Bad men, mostly," Cory clarified, somewhat certain that she was right.

Jess eyed Augie with something like hope. "Does that make a difference?"

"Depends on whether you ask for forgiveness," Augie said.

His hope turned to hardness. "What if I'm not sorry?"

Augie's lips thinned, but he'd expected that Jess Carson would be a tough sell and turned his attention to Cory, who dismissed him with his own church's rules.

"I'm told that God hasn't got much use for a divorced woman."

"Too bad, old man," Eduardo joked, "you're surrounded by sinners."

They shuddered to think about what Eduardo had done and though they knew he was joking; they exchanged glances, knowing that he was right.

"We had better live our lives to the fullest then," Cory said, "while we can."

Jess nodded in agreement but didn't dare imagine what that might look like.

Once Eduardo had a fire going, Cory was drawn to the large copper coffee pot he pulled from his pack. The pot had three handles, including one with a wooden grip on which his initials were engraved.

"Good lord," she ran her fingers along the thin chain that attached the lid, "where did you get such a lovely thing?"

"It's not his," Augie complained, "he stole it from the saddle bag belonging to a highwayman who held us up not too long ago."

Eduardo grinned and lifted the pot for all of them to see. "He just happened to have the same initials as me."

"I suppose I shouldn't ask what happened to the thief," Cory said.

"Best not," Eduardo agreed, "but Augie's always been jealous that I ended up with the coffee pot." He set about measuring the grounds and teased, "Envy is a sin, old man."

She didn't ask any more about the fate of the highwayman, but she wondered about it. It weighed heavy on her mind that she was in the midst of three dangerous men. Well, possibly only two, though it had been her experience that men of God were often the freest with their hands. It also occurred to her that if she and Jess ever located Adam Colter, she could end up traveling once again as the lone woman in their company.

Once they'd eaten supper, she sipped her coffee and nibbled on a dried apple while the men checked their weapons.

She offered an apple to Jess and asked, "When we find your brother, will he be a...a gentleman?"

He laughed. "I promise that you'll be perfectly safe from Adam. He has terrible taste in women."

Jess had an irritating way of making her blush and she hid her face as she laid out her bedroll between him and Augie. Eduardo sat in the center of their little circle with a rifle on his lap.

"Wake me for a watch," Jess instructed him and then laid down beside Cory.

Augie was already snoring. She nudged him onto his side and then stared for a long time at the stars, feeling small and exposed.

To pass the time, Cory contemplated the many sides of Jess Carson. Dangerous, impetuous, protective, and driven. Could a man like that be loving as well? She chided herself for even pondering the notion. He confused her every now and then with his brazen talk but overall he was focused, rightfully so, on their survival and on his mission to find Adam Colter. She silently argued with her more romantic self that she was bound to nothing more than their mission and promised not to get caught up in anything else. A wave of loneliness passed through her, but she convinced herself that lonely or not, it would be a strange, but comfortable life, and then drifted off.

Beside her Jess watched her sleep until his eyelids wouldn't stay open any longer.

Jess was startled awake in the middle of the night by the sound of a high-pitched squeal, and he found Eduardo poised to throw a carcass off the rise.

"Was it a javalina?"

Eduardo turned and showed him a ghoul's head in one hand and its body in the other. Jess gritted his teeth. "Dammit. How many of them do you think there are?"

"One is too many," Eduardo grumbled.

Jess noticed when they swapped the watch that Eduardo laid down but never closed his eyes.

The others woke bleary and creaky, just before dawn to the smell of extra strong coffee brewing in Jess's small tin pot. He filled Cory's cup and turned her around so she could see the fiery pink and orange streaks across the horizon.

She gasped, "I'll never get used to these incredible sunrises."

His chest puffed out a little and joked, "I arranged

this one just for you."

She sipped her coffee in despair as the promise she'd made to herself the night before evaporated with the morning mist.

Once packed up and on their way, Cory convinced Priscilla to ride up beside Eduardo.

"Can you teach me some Spanish words?" She asked.

"No, he cannot." Augie chuckled as Eduardo glared back at him. "He only pretends to be a Mexican who speaks little English so he doesn't have to talk to people he doesn't want to."

Eduardo is a genius, Jess thought.

"He gets himself into trouble, and I got to get him out," Eduardo thumbed back at Augie, "but I don't have to yammer on. Like some."

"His real name is Edgar Martin." Augie explained.

Cory studied his features and declared, "Eduardo suits you better."

Eduardo shrugged. "My father could have been Mexican for all I know but out here," he gestured to the open desert, "you get to choose who you are."

Cory liked the sound of that very much, but Jess grunted in disagreement. He'd lived his entire life in the west and was pretty sure that his current situation had not been left up to him. In fact, he could remember few situations where he'd ever had the freedom to choose.

Their path followed a tributary of the river that eventually dwindled to a muddy wash about five miles outside of Phoenix. The horses were hot and there were only a few puddles to drink from, so they dismounted to walk for a while.

Cory thought it eerily quiet as she dipped her handkerchief in the dirty water and wiped it across the back of her neck. There were no birds in the trees and the vast desert seemed to be swiftly closing in around them. Dabbing the handkerchief along her throat, she let her head fall back and tried to catch a bit of the breeze. Through the fluttering of the leaves she nearly missed Foley's sinewy limbs blending into the branches as he hovered over them, but from the corner of her eye caught the turquoise glint off the strand of beads dangling from his neck.

She slowly made her way to Priscilla and lifted the saddle blanket so Jess and Eduardo could see that she intended to pull the shotgun from the scabbard.

Their backs stiffened. "What do you see?"

Her voice was barely a whisper, "Foley is in the trees."

"Shit," the men said in unison.

Jess pulled the knife from its sheath on his thigh and he, Eduardo and Augie drew their pistols, scanning the skyline until a loud blast jolted their attention back to Cory.

She'd caught a ghoul leaning against a stump, sucking the marrow out of what looked to her like a shin bone. She didn't want to think about where the bone came from, but she doubted it had been a donation.

Cory had never fired a shotgun, but her stepfather once woefully proclaimed himself cursed to have only daughters, so she'd tried to please him on many occasions by tagging along while he hunted pheasant. The gun was heavier than she expected and when she blew the ghoul off the stump end over end, the butt recoiled into her shoulder, knocking her down hard into a puddle on her backside.

Before Jess could get to her, Foley leapt from the tree. They hit the ground, rolled and sprang back to their feet. The knife shifted its weight to the right, startling Jess but guiding his hand to slash in a wide arc, forcing Foley back and on the defensive.

Foley still had the brakeman's club, and his limbs were long enough that when he swung it, Jess was only just able to leap out of the way. Even if the knife was somehow helping him—a fact he would not yet allow himself to accept—Jess knew that he and Foley would just end up dancing around until one of them tired out, probably him. So he tucked his shoulder and charged, slamming his body into Foley's ribcage while plunging Mark's knife into his chest.

The attack excited Foley as much as it enraged him. He yanked on the back of Jess's hair with a savage grunt and the feel of the serrated knife sawing through his sternum as Jess fell backward thrilled Foley even though it nearly felled him. Nearly.

Cory rose to her knees as two more ghouls sprinted out of the trees toward Augie. She hoisted the shotgun to her shoulder and fired again, but the first ghoul she'd shot tackled her from behind and forced her, face down, into one of the mud puddles.

Foley kicked Jess in the ribs, picked up his club and headed for Cory, who was trying, mostly without success, to keep the dirty water out of her lungs. When Foley tossed the ghoul aside, she scrambled away on all fours, but he pulled her feet from underneath her and she collapsed to her stomach.

As he dragged her face down through the wash, a

dark long-haired man seemingly came from out of nowhere to jump him from behind. Foley dropped his club when he fell, and the long-haired man seized it up, connecting across Foley's shoulders with a sharp crack.

Foley howled as his brittle bones fractured, "What are you doing here, Mark?"

"Mark?" Jess wheezed. He hauled himself up and staggered toward them until he caught sight of Cory lying motionless in the sand.

Chapter Thirteen

"Be still!"

They all turned in the direction of Eduardo's shout and then Jess's heart sank. While chasing one of the ghouls, Eduardo and Augie had agitated a large patch of lightly packed sand that floated atop a subterranean section of the river. Stinking gasses rose from the muck as the earth began to wobble under their feet.

"Get away from there!" Jess hollered over his shoulder, still moving toward Cory. Again, out of nowhere, another stranger appeared from behind them and scooped her up. Her hair was matted across her face, but Jess could tell even from that distance that she was breathing.

The new stranger clearly had Cory's well-being in mind, but something snapped in Jess at the sight of her in another man's arms.

Foley smiled to himself. Even through the pain of his broken bones he could feel the simmering rage. Jess wanted to kill the man—a man he didn't even know.

Jess looked from Cory and the stranger to Augie and Eduardo and back again. He would stifle his irrational jealousy, for now. Water was beginning to pool around Augie's calves as the reverend against the pull of the quicksand

Jess dropped to his knees and crawled in their

direction, careful not to upset the ground around himself. By the time he reached them, Eduardo was knee deep but yanking up on Augie's legs, freeing him enough for Jess to pull him out.

Water soaked into his Jess's pants, and he felt the tug on his body getting stronger, but he took Augie under the arms, and with one great heave they rolled away.

The suction grew more powerful as Eduardo began to flail with panic. The quicksand had reached chest high and the more he moved the faster he sank.

"I'm coming for you!" Jess tore down a long mesquite branch and carefully began to navigate the sludge until an arm roughly pulled him back.

The stranger who had carried Cory to safety was at his side with a rope. "I will tie it to the horse," he said.

Jess secured his branch to the other end of the rope as the Frenchman, *Frenchman? Seriously?* ran back to tether them.

"Grab it!" He instructed, but Eduardo had managed to get one of his arms buried and missed the stick. Jess threw it again, but Eduardo was using his free hand to frantically wipe the sand from under his chin. Jess ran toward him with the rope and instantly sank to his ankles.

The Frenchman yelled, "Hold on!" and guided the horse forward.

Jess was out of breath, and panic closed around his heart as the sand rose over his knees. He held on to the rope and slowly moved his legs back and forth until he could fall forward and let the horse do the rest of the work to pull him out.

The Frenchman hauled him to safety, and they

watched helplessly as, in seconds, the undertow dragged Eduardo completely down. It took both of them to stop Augie from running to where Eduardo was buried and when they finally had him subdued, all three collapsed, shivering and coated in crusted sand.

"No!" Cory scrambled toward them and gathered the grieving Augie in her arms.

Other than when Betty ruined his life, Jess didn't think he'd ever been more furious. He jerked away from the Frenchman and stumbled toward Foley and Mark with his pistol drawn.

Mark held the club poised over Foley, saying, "Carson doesn't know what's going on here."

"Do not interfere with my hunt," Foley spat and angled one of his long legs out, sweeping Jess's feet from underneath him. Jess fired three times before landing on his back, but Foley only flinched, not even clutching his chest where blood barely trickled from the bullet holes. He leaned over Jess, stepped a foot on his collar bone, and with a smile pulled a foot long giant desert centipede from his sleeve. He let its segmented body slither between his fingers and then brought it so close to Jess's face that its many legs brushed against his jaw.

It was a strange game that Foley had to play. He had to wear down his prey, but not too much. Carson must remain sharp, but always off balance. Foley pinched the centipede's head to show Jess its fangs, and said, "I hear that the bite from one of these big ones will paralyze a full-grown man."

"Go ahead." Jess gritted his teeth, determined not to look away. "If you don't do it, I'm going to kill you as slowly as I possibly can."

Foley held up the centipede and licked his lips, then he practically danced himself face to face with Mark, and in a sing-song voice said, "He knows now."

He shook the beaded necklace he wore at Mark and added, "*You* should have known better than to get involved."

Mark stood his ground but sweat poured from his temples. Though Jess had never met the man before, he recognized the fear in his eyes.

A ghoul trapped neck deep squealed from the quicksand, capturing everyone's attention. Foley swore and then whispered a few words under his breath. As the spell released his spirit into the ether, the ghoul's head fell forward, and he went limp as the gritty earth swallowed him up.

It was a shame, Foley thought. He was losing ghouls faster than he could make them, and there was little time to enslave new spirits. Mark's interference ruined his plans for this encounter but had delivered a priceless detail. Jess Carson, while particularly fond of the woman, would risk his life for anyone he called a friend. Foley flicked the centipede at Jess before using his favorite trick to disappear in a cloud of dust.

The centipede slithered over Jess's leg and when it dropped in the dirt, Cory stabbed it with his knife, wiped the blade in the grass and handed it back to him.

"You're letting him get away?" Jess rasped to Mark as Cory and the Frenchman hauled him to his feet. He was covered in dirt and sweat, his lungs were on fire, and he could barely breathe. He'd been caught on the back foot three times by Foley and now a man was dead. The shame of being bested so badly while having no clue as to why fueled a fury in him directed at everyone there but Cory.

She kicked away the centipede corpse with the toe of her boot and positioned herself at his side when he aimed his pistol at Mark and pulled back the hammer. "You'd better tell me who you are and what the hell is going on."

"Easy boy, this here is Mark Chisolm," Augie said, wiping a hand across his tear-streaked face.

"And that's René Auclair," Cory said in his ear, "we met in Prescott."

She turned to René. "How did you find us? What are you doing here?"

He smirked at her. "Still asking questions, I see."

"What do you want to know?" Mark asked Jess.

Jess never lowered his gun, but his shoulders sagged with exhaustion. His brain swam with grief and guilt and confusion and fear and rage, and the only thing clear to him was that Mark was at the center of it all.

Mark could sense that Jess was struggling with where to begin so he said, "How about I tell you something you *need* to know."

"What's that?"

Mark flipped the club in his hand a couple of times and then said, "Foley is my brother."

* * *

"I'm sorry, Augie." Jess would have rather kept his distance, but the old preacher deserved better than cowardly silence. Maybe by looking in the face of the man who'd let his friend and protector die, Augie could somehow see how truly awful Jess felt about it.

"I don't know how much harder you could have

tried to save his life," Augie gave a short sad laugh, "besides, he didn't like to admit it, but I'd already saved his soul."

Jess arched an eyebrow and Augie said, "Yes, sir, Eduardo was my biggest success story," he eyed Jess up and down, "so far."

Augie would miss Eduardo but no more than he missed all the other friends he'd lost during a life that he believed had already been way too long.

The deep crow's feet around August Ortega's tired eyes were the only physical features that belied his advanced age. He moved a little slow but, as Eduardo had often pointed out it was usually just to get sympathy. He felt that his main purpose in life was to bring as many souls to God as he could, but a close second was to be there for Mark Chisolm, whose father had been Augie's dearest friend ever and one of the first of his friends to die.

Mark also sent a fair number of souls to God, but not of their own free will. Augie would have preferred that Mark take the path to salvation, but he was a complicated fellow. He often thought of Dante and wondered if there were also circles in Heaven. Perhaps there was one a few rungs down where those with thorny natures and questionable provenances could live out eternity, not drowning in a lake of fire, but in something more like a perpetually uncomfortable sweat.

Augie believed that God used people like Mark, and probably Jess, to do his dirtiest work, so it seemed unfair to throw them in Hell before at least giving them some kind of trial. Augie couldn't testify in such a trial; he would never lie under oath and there were some truths he'd been witness to that would not necessarily help the defendants' cases.

He and Jess found the others cleaning up by the shore. They'd doubled back a bit to where the river ran full so they could rest and gather their wits. Jess approached Mark, who raised a hand to stop him as he opened his mouth to speak.

Mark was weathered, but not aged and Jess knew without asking that he was a man who'd seen too much. The dark circles around his dark eyes gave him an uncanny appearance, but Jess acknowledged that if Foley was his family, it was likely the result of perpetual distress.

"Foley is a necromancer," Mark said, "but you probably had that figured out."

"He makes those ghouls," Cory agreed. She'd rinsed her entire self, clothes and all, in the river and was stretched out on the bank to dry.

"Low vibrational parasites," Mark clarified, "they're possessing their own dead bodies, but they don't even know that. They rely on him for everything, so they do whatever he tells them to do."

"Like crashing a god damned train," Jess snarled.

Cory wrapped her arms around her middle, remembering Foley's wicked multi-layered grin. "He looks like a dead thing himself."

"There's a curse on him, a curse that he's now shared with you. Foley keeps himself alive using black magic," Mark explained, "he's a scavenger and a thief, merging spells and rituals he's gathered from different cultures with his own to try to break that curse. The closest he's ever managed is The Hunt."

"The Hunt?"

"He needs your blood, Jess—all of it—to finish the

ritual that will keep him alive for a few years more."

Jess didn't bother asking what Foley intended to do with his blood.

"He was already delusional when my people banished him," Mark continued, "but the curse they put on him has turned him into a madman. He could simply murder you, but The Hunt has become part of the spell—it thrills him to track you, to wear you down, to destroy you."

"Why me?"

"You must have impressed him in some way."

"So, it's just my bad luck?"

"Better he wants to fight you than turn you into one of those fiends," René offered.

Jess shuddered at the thought. "Why doesn't he just fight me now?"

"Significant events that have an impact on a man stay in his blood, and the more heightened your state of anger and fear, the longer the spell works," Mark said.

"Jesus." Jess picked up a stick, snapped it in two and threw it down.

"What if I don't want to play his game?"

"Right," Cory said, "We're going to be busy looking for Jess's brother, Adam Colter. Maybe you've heard of him?"

"I know you've heard of him," Jess said, conscious of the letter in his pocket, "but how did you hear about me?"

"Clemente Hinojosa told me your story."

Jess's mouth fell open.

"I showed up to the ranch right after Adam Colter left you there."

"I don't remember that." Jess's early memories of

the ranch were little more than a pain-soaked blur.

"I'm not surprised," Mark said, "you were bleeding to death at the time. In fact, I'm surprised that you're standing in front of me right now."

"I don't know if it's your brother or not, but I heard of a fellow who goes by the name of AJ Colter." Augie interrupted. "He helped a family I know across the mountains on his way to work the silver mines in Tombstone."

Jess and Cory exchanged looks.

"Rides an Appaloosa, I think," Augie added as an afterthought.

"That's him. That's Adam." Jess bounced on the balls of his feet and turned to Cory. "Are you coming with me to Tombstone?"

Mark made a face at Augie, who shrugged and said, "Well, that's what I heard."

"This is yours." Jess began to untie the sheath from around his thigh. He hadn't made it to Phoenix, but he'd delivered the knife to Mark. It was the first decent lead he'd had on Adam's whereabouts in six months and Tombstone was far away from Foley. He held the knife out, but Mark wouldn't take it.

"Foley won't stop until you're dead," he cast a glance at Cory, "he's already made her a target too, do you want the same for Adam?"

Jess stomped around the group, he couldn't believe it. "You can't do this to me."

"I'm trying to help you," Mark assured him, "Foley will follow wherever you go, and you can't fight him on your own." He put his hand on Jess's shoulder, "Help me stop my brother, and I'll help you find yours. I promise."

Chapter Fourteen

Cory took Jess's hand in hers and, looking into his eyes asked, "What do you want to do?"

Instinctively, he looked to his left but of course Adam wasn't there to advise him. Adam wasn't there but his brother was so close now that he could almost feel his presence as acutely as he felt his absence. He returned Cory's gaze and then looked at Foley's club in Mark's hand. He was afraid, but he wasn't alone.

"This affects you too," he said pulling Cory aside, "What's your opinion?"

She'd been thinking about it since Augie showed up at the restaurant. While she hadn't known Foley was Mark's brother, she was certain even then that they wouldn't easily be rid of him. And she'd be lying if she said she wasn't damn curious about Mark and *his people,* so she chose her words carefully.

"He can't do it alone Jess, and neither can we. I don't believe he would lie about helping us find Adam."

"It's obvious that Foley hates him," Jess argued, "and he can't help find anyone if he's dead."

"The same could be said for us," she reminded him.

Jess curled and uncurled his fists. Adam was just out of reach. Again. For a few minutes he'd thought that he could escape this ugly predicament and get back to his old life, but they were right, and his old life seemed farther away than ever.

Cory gave his hand a comforting squeeze and then he realized that she had been missing from that old life, and he was so conflicted that he could hardly bear to think any more about it. What he had to think about were their next moves.

"Foley is kicking our asses, especially mine," he told Mark, "so, how do we beat him? "Do I need to hire a witch or something?"

"Not a witch," Mark answered, "we need a bitch."

They blinked at him.

"We have to visit my mother."

Though he was dead serious, Mark gave them a jovial smile. It was the first time they'd seen the mysterious man display any kind of emotion. It was disarming, but he then so enthusiastically shook both Jess and Cory's hands that they could physically feel a shift in their relationship with him.

Now knowing that Mark was related to a sorcerer, Cory figured that he too must have some kind of mystical inclinations so she held on to his hand for a second longer than she should have. She received no vision, only a solid sense of his sincerity.

"This is still yours." Jess handed him the knife, but Mark turned it down.

"Keep it for now," he said, "you'll be needing it."

Jess noticed that René flicked a similar, but smaller knife in his hand and wondered what could have possibly brought the two of them together.

* * *

René curled his lip as Cory stowed the shotgun in the

scabbard on her saddle. She could not shoot it with anything like skill, but he had no doubt that someone like Carson would think nothing of giving her lessons, further degrading her sophistication.

Jess plucked her new hat off the ground and patted it on her head. "Don't forget this."

"A woman like you should be wearing the latest fashions from Paris," René said low in her ear.

She took a step back, smoothed her still damp split skirt and adjusted her hat. "Fashion isn't very practical out here I'm afraid."

"Which is my point," he said, "I don't understand why you would want to—"

She cut him off. "It is perfectly acceptable for you to be mysterious but not for me?"

"Since we met, I have felt nothing but the desire to tell you everything," he assured her.

Even so, Cory noticed that he did no such thing.

Though Priscilla held still enough, she stomped in place, letting her displeasure be known, much like Jess, who's expression was grim while watching René hold Cory steady as she swung into the saddle.

With tailored clothes and long lean muscles, René appeared more polished than the rugged men she'd encountered out west, but Cory did not think him particularly handsome. There was something alluring about him though. He was obviously just as dangerous as the others, but she wasn't afraid that he would hurt her—not physically anyway.

* * *

Cory found herself obsessing over her telegram as their

party travelled to Augie's town.

"I just know Suzannah has been up to something dangerous since you left," she said to René, "and you promised to protect her."

René sighed and glanced back at Mark. "At this time, he needs me more than she does...you need me too."

Cory lowered her eyelids. "I *am* grateful for what you did back there, and for what you did in Prescott." She looked up at him then. "Why is it that you always seem to know when I'm in trouble?"

René caught Jess's icy stare and returned one of his own before leaning close to her. "Because chére, you are always in trouble."

Jess had no idea what they were talking about and that vexed him beyond reason. He turned to Augie and said, "Who the hell is that guy?"

"Don't know much about him, but if Mark trusts him, he's a good man to have around."

Jess sniffed.

"Not that René is a good man," Augie clarified, "but Mark has a way of finding the best of the worst," he gave Jess a look, "and making good use of their, um, talents."

Jess ran his hand along the hilt of the knife strapped to his thigh. He'd found it in himself to saw the head off a ghoul with it. What had René been capable of doing with his?

The Frenchman hung back to meet Mark at the rear of their procession. They spoke low for a few moments and then Mark nodded and slapped his shoulder before René rode off in the opposite direction.

Jess had been pleased that there was no tearful

goodbye between Cory and the Frenchman, in fact, René never said goodbye at all. Still Jess was surly on the rest of the ride to Augie's town.

Bored by the silence of the men, Cory plucked berries off the cedar trees they passed. How could they spend hours upon hours with no conversation?

She tossed one of the berries at Jess. It bounced off his chin and landed in his lap, but he brushed it away with a scowl, glancing up at the trees but never at her. She tossed another one and another one and only after she threw the entire handful did he realize that it was her.

"Hey, that stings!" He mocked a yelp and flicked one back to her, unable to hide his smile at her giggle.

She took off her glove and held out her hand. He was a bit confused by the gesture, but he did the same and felt a flutter in his belly, a brief flash of a future with her zipping through his mind. But then he thought about what they were likely to face in the future and the flutter migrated up to become a tightening in his chest.

* * *

The blood of a wolf simmered in a clay pot atop one of the flat rocks situated around the fire pit. It was not ideal, but as Foley dipped in his beads, he recalled how fiercely the animal had fought him. It would be enough for now.

He let the beads air dry before securing the strand around his neck. Foley's remaining ghouls chewed their way through the carcass while he laid back on the grass. He pondered the peace Jess Carson was able to find on the banks of a river, but the sound of the Agua Fria rushing by only fueled his own roiling impatience.

There was no other option in his weakened state but to rest while the wolf's blood worked to knit his broken bones together. The spell worked quickly but it was never quite a perfect fit, and the pain would be with him for years to come.

Mark had a lot to answer for and someday Foley would deal with him. Someday, when the curse was broken.

Mark was good at hampering his progress, an annoyance that Foley had learned to factor into every hunt. Although there were some occasions, depending on how wicked the prey turned out to be where Mark utilized his human ability to justify even the most violent of deaths.

For some reason this time his brother had taken a special interest in Carson and the woman. *Some reason?* No, Mark never did anything without *good* reason and that meant Foley's instincts were dead on when he'd selected his target.

It occurred to him once that family blood might be the missing ingredient he needed to break the curse. After all, it was family who did this to him, but after ingesting his brother's blood during a fight with Mark decades ago, he learned that his family's blood was nothing but poison. One by one Foley's organs had festered with infection for weeks at a time, setting back his progress by years.

It was likely that his mother, knowing her son would seek revenge, considered that detail when she devised her spell. Mark was only half-blood so Foley could only imagine what his fate would have been if he'd gone after her.

Initially, his mother had been content to let Foley practice his art in whatever way he wanted, as long as it didn't interfere with her project at the time which was torturing Mark's father. Foley had never been briefed on the elder Chisolm's offense, but she'd probably long forgotten it anyway. Still, the man kept her occupied and out of Foley's business until the incident with the rancher.

His mother was, if nothing else, a survivor, and when given the ultimatum, it took her longer to concoct the necessary spell than it did for her to decide whether or not to sacrifice her son. To her credit, the spell was magnificent and as his days were spent suffering, they were also spent with him wavering between intense hatred of the woman and the utmost respect for her skill. She'd even bewitched the air around them. He was so relaxed at the time that he took the drink from her without question and sipped greedily throughout their conversation.

"You are vain and reckless," she'd told him.

Even more than she knew. He had thought himself like a god, but the Other Side already had gods. Gods who were indifferent to his practices until the humans came looking for revenge. The odd goblin disappearance could be overlooked, but to kidnap a human—a powerful rancher—for experimentation was beyond the pale.

"And you are not reckless?" He'd argued.

She began to caress a creosote bush, plucking off a handful dead leaves as she spoke.

"I am not so arrogant that I do not appreciate my dependence on this Side until the day comes when I can burn it down as I leave it."

"I don't want to leave." He could not imagine doing so.

"But you must, so that I can stay." A Gila monster the size of a dog ambled to her side just then as she raised her hands high over her head, whispering the words to activate the spell. "You require human bodies for your sorcery, so go to their Side and live among them, be one of them, learn their ways and," at this she smiled, "face their justice."

Confused, he stumbled alongside as she dropped the leaves in a line that lead to a deep pocket in the canyon wall, a known portal to the human Side. He began to suspect her intention but thought that surely even she would not banish her own child.

Foley wiped the back of his hand across his forehead as his body tried to force her potion out through his oozing pores. And only then, as the Gila monster flicked a thin flame off its venomous tongue to ignite the dried leaves, did he grasp the depth of her betrayal. The leaves lit up like a line of blasting powder engulfing Foley, who was now coated with her flammable potion. He'd become a seven-foot fireball, flicked easily by the Gila monster's thick tail through the portal to the human Side.

He learned quickly that he could not survive among them. They were frightened of his appearance, angered by his habits and more than once he was imprisoned for crimes that he still did not understand. Gems that lay in the sand for the taking on his Side were somehow precious to the humans. It was only after absconding with some healing turquoise that he was able to put a spell on himself. He could not break his mother's curse, but he found that the healing beads, once soaked in the blood of the Navajo warrior he fought for them, would extend his life. For a while.

It was mother's little joke, her nod to his necromantic powers.

But this hunt could, no, it would be the last. Somehow, he now believed that Jess Carson's blood would break the curse, and that Mark would be weakened after losing his chosen friends. Relieving himself of his brother would be the first indulgence enjoyed after the new beginning.

He began to feel the healing rush of the wolf's blood and not a minute too soon for he could not afford to let Jess and his companions gather in safety for too long.

Away from the fire, ears pinned back and growling, the wolf's mate sat back on its haunches.

Chapter Fifteen

"There's no hotel, but I'll make space for the two of you in the church."

Augie led them up five uneven steps with no railing to a small, weathered shack. There was no steeple or bell, but a tarnished brass cross took up nearly half the front door, in case anyone was unsure of where they were.

Inside, a second, smaller cross carved from mesquite hung on the far wall behind a pulpit. There was only enough room for two long benches, and a stack of hymnals sat on the end of one with a stack of slates at the end of the other.

"The church doubles as a school," Augie explained when Jess picked up a slate.

"You have kids here?" Jess wondered, thinking of how desolate it was.

"Ten kids," Mark answered.

"Nine," Augie corrected.

"Oh, yeah...I forgot about that."

Jess did not want to hear about *that*. "So, no hotel?"

He didn't bother to hide his annoyance with the arrangement, but Augie was unmoved.

"The town doesn't want a hotel," he said, and looked from Jess to Cory adding, "You're not married, but folks won't run their mouths about Cory if you're staying in the church."

"I don't suppose they'd trouble themselves with the state of Mr. Carson's virtue," Cory snarked.

Jess sighed. There was no arguing her point. "Does this town have a restaurant? Or are the people here sustained by their morals?"

Mark chuckled. "This is certainly no mining camp, but you'll find that there's a fairly loose definition of morals around here. The preacher tends to focus on how he thinks it should be and not on how it is." He put his arm around Cory and led her and Jess to the door. "You'll get a decent meal at Marco's down Main Street, on the left."

Marco Salazar's restaurant was in an adobe building just large enough for its two long tables. His wife, Doli, had adorned the tables with terra cotta vases full of wildflowers that were evenly spaced atop delicate lace runners. The kitchen consisted of a hot fire and a comal under the pergola out back.

One table was empty, but a handful of customers were gathered at the other. There was room for the two of them there and Cory did not wish to be antisocial, so she seated herself at the end. Antisocial was always Jess's preference but he sat down across from her and smiled at Mrs. Salazar who brought them a plate of warm tortillas.

The locals didn't appear that interested in Cory's attempt at pleasantries, so she focused on her dinner of roasted chicken, squash and beans. She'd never tried squash and when she commented to Mrs. Salazar that it was delicious, Marco came in and personally offered her a bowl of ice cream. Jess was not an ice cream lover, but he enjoyed watching her devour it until someone at the other end nearly knocked over the table.

A man far too clumsy to do so was using his entire body to tell what was, as far as Jess could make out, the biggest pack of lies he'd ever heard. And he'd heard some whoppers. Jess lowered his head over his dinner but grunted his disapproval just loud enough to catch the man's attention, which only encouraged him to engage his entire vocal range as well.

Evidently on the way back from a trip to Phoenix, the storyteller had seen a huge cluster of brightly colored orbs lingering over the desert.

"When I first looked up, they were bouncin' all over the sky," he described them by whirling and punching his fists in the air, "then they lined up like little soldiers and just stayed there."

"Where are they now?" A man at the table asked between bites of beans.

"Well, they headed south and disappeared."

"Asa Daggett, you seen some stars is all," the man laughed.

"No!" Asa was indignant, "these lights were closer than stars. I think maybe it was angels."

Jess snorted, and Cory kicked him underneath the table.

Asa glared in their direction and continued, "Anyway, I must have wandered for hours following them."

"How do you know?" Doli asked.

Asa furrowed his brows and took on a faraway look, as if he'd lost a memory that might just have been too terrible to recall. "Be-because," he stammered, "my boots were tattered and my feet were bleeding when I got back to the wagon."

"That don't sound like angels to me. You sure you didn't take a fall?"

"I was in a disoriented state for sure, but I did not fall."

"Wasn't it last year, about this time," the other man tapped a finger on his chin, "that Del Davis said he saw something like that?"

"Del Davis is always drunk," Asa argued, "and you all know I don't drink...not anymore."

"How'd you find your way back to the wagon in the middle of the desert at night?"

Asa shook his head. "I don't remember anything after seeing the lights."

Jess would have expected a wild story about a couple of uppity strangers who were run out of town for not knowing their place. As a perpetual stranger in town, he was used to that kind of loud passive bullying, and he'd heard some version of that story a hundred times. If Asa was trying to scare him off, he'd have to come up with a hell of a lot more than strange lights in the sky. Not that he could confidently discount the story altogether. It was probably bullshit but given what they'd already seen, he had to admit that anything was possible. Still, he balked at the nature of the warning.

Sensing that he was losing everyone's interest, Asa said, "We should form a party and go check it out. You can see for yourselves." He slapped his hand down on the table, jostling what was left of Jess's dinner along with what was left of his nerves.

He stood up and threw his napkin on the table. "Do you mind?"

"What's your problem, stranger?" Asa moved closer to Jess.

"We've had a long ride, and I'd like a quiet dinner."

"Well, this ain't a quiet type of place, so maybe you should leave."

"Maybe you should shut your mouth."

Here we go again, Cory thought to herself. Unwilling to waste her ice cream, she took another giant bite before gathering enough coins from her purse to pay for their dinner and any subsequent damages.

"Thank you very much," she whispered to Mrs. Salazar, who gave her a sympathetic look, "everything was wonderful."

"Let it go, Asa." Their heads all turned in Marco's direction and the sound of his lever action as he cocked it. "And you," he said to Jess, "on your way."

Outside Cory complained, "If you do that in every restaurant we visit, I'm going to have to learn to eat faster."

"I was in the right, Cory."

"Yes, well you know he's going to come after us and if you thought you were tired before...oh, look here he is now."

Jess moved Cory behind him as Asa emerged from the restaurant, ready for a fight.

"I'm not in the mood," Jess warned him.

"Why hasn't it occurred to you that no one around here cares what you want?" Asa had no sooner finished that sentence when he paled a bit and said, "but I'll let it slide today."

Jess felt a hand on his shoulder and looked over to see Mark, who said, "Nothin' to worry about, Asa."

Asa nodded and rushed back to the restaurant

hollering something to the others inside about having taken care of the problem.

Cory breathed an audible sigh of relief and Jess apologized for bringing her more trouble. "We're outsiders and I ought to have known better."

Mark shook his head. "You're not outsiders when you're with me."

"You'll be safe here," Mark promised, after leading Jess and Cory back to the church.

Augie had stabled their horses and was busy piling their things next to the bedrolls laid out on either side of the pulpit. Jess took over the task and Augie sat down with a groan on one of the benches.

"What the heck have you got in there?" He asked Cory of her tapestry bag.

"Everything."

Cory's voice took on a dreamy quality and Mark watched with interest as her gaze was drawn to the flame from a thin white taper burning atop the preacher's stand. Though Augie was seated, in her mind she saw him lighting the candle, kneeling in front of the cross and mumbling a prayer for his new friends.

The vision evaporated when Augie stood and blew out the candle. "I'll be out back," he grumbled.

"Out back?" If Augie were going to stand watch, Jess wanted to arrange for a wakeup when it was his turn.

"He and Eduardo built two small houses behind the church last year," Mark said.

"Two?"

"Side by side," Mark chuckled, "Eduardo said he

didn't mind looking *after* the old man all the time, but he didn't want to look *at* him all the time."

"Eduardo drew some pictures of the angels that I want to keep," Augie smiled sadly, "so I'll pack up his place tonight."

"He was an artist?" For some reason Cory wasn't surprised.

"He was something of a renaissance man before we met—wrote poems, drew pictures and shot people for pay."

"Nothing changed after they met," Mark chuckled, "he just started doing it all for Jesus."

He lit a lantern and handed it to Jess, before pushing open the door to leave. "Old Augie will be getting some much-needed rest tonight and I suggest you do the same."

When he was gone, Jess and Cory sat side by side on one of the benches, watching the shadows from the lantern on the wall and enjoying the fact that, at least for the time being, Mark was true to his word, and they were safe.

"Are you alright," she asked.

For a second, he imagined the two of them settled in their own home, reading together by the fire. It was absurd, he knew, and even if she were inclined, the obstacles to such a dream were mounting by the hour. Still, in that moment he allowed himself a bit of hope— something he'd not indulged in since before Betty robbed that bank—and said, "I might be. You?"

It took her a while to answer, but finally she said, "Sometimes I don't think so."

"Like at the restaurant?" He gave her a sheepish smile, "I'll behave from now on."

"You will not." She pushed playfully against him. "I was talking more about ghouls and sorcerers and curses, but strangely," she rested her head on his shoulder, "I'm starting to believe this is where I'm supposed to be. If that's the case, then I guess I am just fine."

Jess was asleep before his body had completely stretched out, but Cory paced the floor. What she'd said to him was only half true. She was where she thought she was supposed to be, but she was not alright, and she didn't know if she ever would be again.

She was afraid for them and when she closed her eyes, no matter how she strained to see it, there was no vision of what their future might hold. "That's not how it works," her mother had said, "you don't get to choose the messages."

The door shrieked loudly as she pushed it open, but looking back she saw that Jess didn't stir. Sleeping in a church, under a cross no less, didn't really bother her. Augie's faith was palpable in that tattered building—something she'd never felt in the gilded big city cathedrals. Even so, she needed some air.

A splinter snagged her split skirt as she settled in on the top step and she considered changing into her new pants, just for the night of course, but then thought better of it. The town was already making judgments about them, and it wouldn't do to borrow more trouble.

"You have a gift."

She should have been startled by Mark's voice in the darkness. But, as was his way, he emerged from the shadows at the foot of the steps making her feel protected rather than vulnerable.

"If gifted is what you want to call it." She worried the snag in her skirt to avoid meeting his eyes, "Cursed and damned are the words I've most commonly heard."

"You think you're damned, based on what other people say? People with far less experience than you?"

She'd been asking herself the same thing for years and the answer was simple.

"They might have less experience, but they have more power." She leaned back on her elbows and studied the stars. "In truth, I envy those who believe without question, but if heaven is lost to someone like me then what is the point?"

"I don't believe...I know," Mark said, "the problem for me is that I don't know why."

She could sense that would become a shared problem and it terrified her. They'd agreed to walk Mark Chisolm's path for long enough to stop Foley, but what then?

"I assume you have gifts at least equal to your brother's," she said, "your family gatherings must be fascinating."

"You'll think differently when you meet my mother."

He climbed the steps past her and opened the door. Frustrated by the not-so-subtle indication that he would not be elaborating; she hesitated before going inside. But he was patient, and she was tired, so he won. As the door closed behind him, she fumed inwardly that once again a man she was supposed to trust had evaded her questions. Evasion seemed to come natural to all men. All but one. One who never tried to hide anything from her except his feelings, and he wasn't very good at that.

Jess slept so hard that he never stirred when she

pulled the blanket over him, which was just as well because she would not have wanted him to hear her cry herself to sleep.

Chapter Sixteen

After an uneventful breakfast, chaperoned by Augie at the only other restaurant, and on the other side of town from Marco's, Jess began to question Mark's plan.

"I thought we were going to get some answers from his mother."

"I wouldn't be too anxious for that visit," Augie advised.

If he were honest, Jess wasn't looking forward to it either. He *was* interested in exploring the area though. "Is that a river I hear?"

Augie nodded. "The runoff from these mountains feeds the river and a creek that flows over the waterfall, which is probably what you're hearing. We were blessed with a wet winter, so the falls have been strong lately."

"Then I'm going fishing," Jess announced, and headed back to the church for his pole.

Augie blanched. "I'll go with you."

"I don't want you to go with me."

"As a matter of fact, I don't want to go, but that river has some eccentricities that you need to watch out for."

Of that Jess had no doubt but he would have liked some time alone. Still, he'd been less friendly with Augie than he meant to be. Cory would have made polite conversation as they walked so in her honor he tried his best by asking about a boarded-up building at the end of the street.

"That's the jail," Augie said. He wasn't keen on chit chat either, particularly about the jail.

"Where's the Sheriff?"

"There was an...incident a while back and we haven't really seen him since."

"Haven't *really* seen him?" Jess blinked at him. "That's just great."

They walked the rest of the way in silence until Jess made an audible gasp when they reached their destination. The water rushed over the falls in three tiers pooling at the bottom in a natural granite tank that spilled over into the river. Tall grasses grew in between the enormous flat rocks scattered along the bank, one of which, situated under a palo verde tree, he chose as his spot.

"When are you going to marry that girl?" Augie asked out of nowhere.

Jess's heart lurched. The preacher had so casually mentioned what he barely dared to hope for that it made him irrationally angry.

"Don't go planting seeds that won't get watered. Besides we've only known each other for a few days."

"A lot has happened in those days," Augie argued while arranging a stack of sugar cubes artfully atop the rock.

When Jess gaped at the sugar, he explained, "You have to make it clear that your intentions are friendly." He noted that Jess's expression had soured with talk of marriage and added, "Well, at least my intentions are friendly." He stretched out his legs and tried another tactic. "You'll be safer traveling as a married couple. It's cheaper and there will be fewer, uh, questions."

The glint of something across the river caught Jess's eye. It didn't shimmer like the water, but it was bright. "What's over there?"

"There's nothing but danger on the Other Side."

"Really? Just on the other side of the river?"

"This town is loaded with portals to the Other Side of *existence* and that's one of them."

"Oh yeah?" Jess was so grateful to have changed the subject from marriage that he didn't even care that Augie's explanation was insane. "What exactly lives on the Other Side?"

Augie rubbed his stubble while working out how much to tell. At last, he decided that a short version of the whole truth wouldn't hurt. "The old gods and their kind were put on the Other Side when the humans took over the world."

Jess could deduce who put them there and he doubted that they went willingly. If it were true, then a whole lot of humans would have a whole lot of rewriting to do.

"Doesn't that create some problems within your belief system?"

"Some."

"But you don't ask questions you don't want the answers to?"

"The answers I do have don't make any sense. If you'll pay attention, what I'm tryin' to get across here is that this place," he opened his arms in a wide gesture to the mountains, "is on the edge between worlds and we who live here have to get along. In your case, it's best to ignore them. Just stay over here because you could run into a goblin...or worse."

"Are goblins like ghouls?"

"Both are awful creatures but there are differences."

"Such as?"

"Ghouls are made, and goblins are born."

"Naturally."

"Nothin' natural about it, so stay over here."

Made versus born was a distinction that Jess felt needed further clarification since he was certain to run into one no matter how hard he tried to stay away, but just then his line bobbed. It was empty when he pulled it up, so he threaded a few more pieces of corn onto the hook.

He stared hard at the glimmer across the river but could never quite figure out what it was.

Augie sensed his curiosity mounting and said, "This town has a lot of...peculiarities, and most people just don't have the fortitude for such things." It was true, but as he said it, Augie had a sinking feeling that Jess and Cory would actually thrive there.

Jess narrowed his eyes. "What happened to the Sheriff?"

"Oh, he'll likely turn up sooner or later."

Since she would rather bite off her own fingertip than sit silently for hours watching Jess cast his line, Cory had stayed behind. Augie preferred that she not be by herself and cursed Eduardo's untimely demise, but in this case, he figured that Jess would require the most supervision and left her with some simple instructions.

He had told her not to wander around aimlessly, so she stepped out of the church with purpose. She wore the only other outfit that she owned, a dark brown skirt paired with her new white linen button-down blouse. Just one petticoat would fit in her tapestry bag so she had to make do, fluffing out the skirt as best as she could and hoping that she looked as smart as she needed to.

Augie made the town sound perilous and otherworldly, but even keenly aware of the eyes peering out at her as she made her way down the eerily empty Main Street, she didn't find the townspeople to be that unusual. Suspicious and judgmental were not characteristics that any one area could lay specific claim to.

All the same, Mark and Augie seemed as comfortable there as they were fighting ghouls in the wild. That such a town bothered to publish a newspaper made her wonder just what news was fit to print, and she'd set out to purchase the latest issue.

Augie also told her not to talk to anyone, but she found the newspaper man, Chester Wilder, to be friendlier than everyone she'd met thus far.

"No paper yet to sell, but as soon as I finish this story," he held up a few handwritten pages, "the first issue will go to press."

She peered at the pages and though she couldn't read everything, she did see her name scribbled on them in several places. "I wouldn't expect that there would be enough news for all this," she gestured to the press, "in such a small town."

He laughed, "Oh, there's plenty, if you know where to look."

Chester had no hair except for wiry gray eyebrows and a matching mustache that grew down to his chin. He kept an unlit pipe clamped between his teeth and, unlike the other men in her party, wore his pants over his boots. His rolled-up shirtsleeves revealed several scars across his sun leathered skin when he reached across the desk to shake her hand.

"What did you do before you were a newspaper man?" She asked, eyeing the scars.

He didn't appear to be self-conscious about it, but he did pull his round glasses down over his nose to give Cory an accusatory stare. "Are you being observant or just nosy?"

"A little of both. But you're living a dream of mine, and I'm curious about what kind of man is led to believe that there would be plenty of news out here in the middle of nowhere."

"Ah," he pushed his glasses to the top of his bald head, "If you're a friend to Mark Chisolm, I think you already know."

She considered that for a moment and then said, "Fair enough. But he's very mysterious, and stingy with his facts."

Chester sat down at his desk and silently dismissed her while pretending to focus on his article. It was no surprise that he would not elaborate about Mark, and even though he was about to print gossip on her, she found that she liked him.

"By the way," she said, "my name is Cory Lindsay, spelled 'ay' not 'ey'."

"Ha!" He was unabashed. "I'll make the correction. Oh, and speaking of mysterious, I've heard there's a telegram for you next door."

"Hmmm," Cory mused, pausing on her way out, "here's a fact for you: I didn't think that anyone knew I was here."

He took some notes and pumped his eyebrows at her. "The more trouble you get into, the better this story will be."

The Post Office clerk was less affable than Chester, offering the minimum amount of conversation required for the transaction. He kept his distance and gave her the side eye while she read her message, as if being a stranger in town were a contagious disease.

Alain suffers a condition. Will visit soon and bring Chloe. Much love, Suzannah.

Oh dear.
"Here's the other one," the clerk said.
"Another one?" Indeed, there was also a message from her young half-sister, Julia.

Angus to marry mean cow Olive Emerson. Miss you. Come home. At least write. Yours, Julia.

Good lord. Olive was Julia's age and once, after learning that Julia had broken her tail bone during a fall down the stairs, Olive told their friends that Julia had been born with a long tail that came off in the accident. She hadn't matured much since, but perhaps Angus would finally get his five sons. Cory was perversely cheered by that thought and made a mental note to share it with Julia as soon as she had time to write a letter.

"Are there no messages for Mr. Jess Carson?"
"Nope, sorry."
She would keep her messages to herself then.

She looked up to ask the clerk when the telegrams had arrived, but he was moving quickly toward the back of the building.

"Good news from home?"

She whirled around to find Mark standing behind her. *Aha.* She held up the papers. "How do they know that I'm here?"

"You didn't answer my question."

Insufferable man. Her lips thinned at first, but then she smiled, "In a strange way yes, it is good news." After considering Suzannah's note and Alain's unknown 'condition', she added, "all of it."

* * *

More irritated by Augie's presence than by the fact that the fish weren't biting, Jess decided to give it up and head back. He wasn't going to get any peace with the reverend reciting all the local oddities.

"You'll hear that there's gold in these mountains, but you'll find a mountain lion before you find any gold," he warned as they approached the church.

"Better to come across a mountain lion than a goblin I suppose," Jess sighed.

"Well, that depends..." Augie started and then noticed Jess eyeing the orange slices laid out at the top of the steps. "Those are for the butterflies. Their tiny teeth will draw more blood than a mosquito."

After all they'd been through, Augie's bizarre warnings were beginning to make perfect sense to Jess and the absurdity of it all made him tired. He caught himself mentally jotting down a note about the butterfly teeth and then leaned against the railing and ran a hand through his hair. He smiled at Augie and then at the town and then at a Monarch that landed nearby. He watched it flitter around the fruit and began to laugh. He first threw his head back and then doubled over, wheezing until Cory and Mark came outside to meet them.

Though they had no idea what he found so funny, Cory had never heard him laugh so hard and it was an infectious, delightful sound. His huge grin lit up his entire face and she couldn't help but join him until from down the street they heard someone calling out for Augie. They all turned at once to see Frank and Violet Gallagher charging up the street.

Frank looked as if he were once a rounder man, but his clothes now hung loose on his frame. Violet followed close on his heels pressing a delicate handkerchief to her lips with one hand and carrying a bundle of dead vegetables in the other.

"Reverend Ortega!" Frank hollered, "Violet says it's getting worse!"

Augie gave Mark a long-suffering look and then took the vegetables from her. "What happened to your carrots, Vi?"

"These were picked this morning," she wailed, "I left them on the table to hang out the laundry and when I came back..." she waved her hand at the gray bunch flopping dead over Augie's fingers.

"Sir, you are bleeding." Cory dug in her pocket and then pressed her own handkerchief to a puncture wound between Frank's left thumb and forefinger.

"I assure you it could have been much worse." He waved away her assistance but kept the handkerchief, wrapping it tightly around his hand.

"I told you both that the town ain't ready for a hotel," Augie said, looking sideways again at Mark, who remained quietly in the shadow of the church's doorway.

"And I told you that it's simply a matter of getting rid of whatever haunts the house."

"Your house is haunted?" Jess found he was less and less interested in the Gallaghers as the moments dragged on.

Frank nodded and turned to face Augie. "I've written to my priest in St. Louis, and he said that when the house is cleansed, we can proceed uninhibited with the construction. You *are* a man of God, are you not?"

August Ortega considered himself to be very close to God, but he was a simple preacher in the middle of nowhere, not a priest, and he had a hard enough time luring the locals into the pews without associating himself with the eviction of an angry spirit. It was his inclination to leave it alone.

He looked everywhere except Frank's eyes, and then Violet began to cry. Cory had doubted Suzannah, and she would not make the same mistake twice. She took Violet by the arm and said, "Show me."

In unison, Jess and Augie let their heads fall back in aggravation, but finally Mark stepped into the light and gestured for them to follow the women, who were already heading for the Gallagher house. Augie tossed the limp carrots aside and again the locals spied out their windows at the newcomers' grim procession through town.

Chapter Seventeen

Main street was sparse compared to Black Canyon City and certainly Prescott. Marco's restaurant was in between the saloon and the general store. Across the street, the bank, the livery stable and two different workshops were on either side of a non-descript building with a large blacked out window facing the street.

"Not exactly booming," Jess noted aloud.

"It will be," Frank said. "A post office just opened up inside the store and that newspaper man from back east—what's his name again?"

"Chester Wilder," Cory replied, earning an exasperated sigh from Augie.

"Wilder. That's it. He tells me he's almost ready to publish the first issue of the Chronicle."

"That will be a quick read," Augie sniffed.

"There's gold in those mountains and the railroad is going to make this town a stop." Frank said, undeterred.

Jess looked at Augie, who said, "Everyone who looks for that gold goes missing."

"Do you know what happened to the Sheriff?" Jess asked Frank. "I'm told he disappeared."

"More like he ran off," Frank clarified, "he wasn't cut out for the job anyway."

Jess wondered if the Sheriff had tried his hand at

gold mining. Even if the man never found a single nugget, the money would have been almost as good as law enforcement.

"This is a beautiful location," Cory mused, "I don't know why more visitors don't flock here, demanding accommodations."

She craned her neck to follow the jagged line of the peaks that loomed over the town and answered her own question. To the casual observer, or one obsessed with profit, the town might seem like any other, but Cory could sense the difference even if she couldn't explain it.

The canyons, so impassable that the river only just snaked its way through, seemed to echo with the warnings scrawled in ancient symbols across their walls. Yellow brittlebrush grew wild over the mountainsides reaching up through the morning mist that lingered in an otherworldly haze over the desert floor, beautifully camouflaging the hazards lurking under every bush— dangers both venomous and enigmatic.

Mark was right, she thought, it was a place best left in the care of those few who understood it.

They were led away from the Main Street business district toward a haphazardly built group of homes scattered more or less in two rows. Temecula Street was literally cut off by an imposing butte, but Agave Street wound itself against the base of a mountain with adobe homes lining each side.

As they approached what was to be the boarding house, Violet shared her own assessment of the place.

"Oh, sure it looks nice enough, but the reality is muddy rutted roads in winter and dry dusty unbreathable hot air in the summer. Reptiles and insects—have you ever seen a scorpion? We have so many..." Her breathing grew labored, and she fanned herself with the handkerchief. "Angry brown pigs and wild dogs..." She paused at the edge of the dirt road as if she would have to force herself to continue.

From that short distance the Gallagher place seemed quite homey with sheets drying on a line, lace curtains fluttering out of the open windows and half a dozen chickens pecking at the ground. Two three-armed saguaros stood like sentries on either side of the property and one of them even hosted the nest of a cactus wren.

But as they closed the gap there were obvious signs of trouble that Frank either could not or would not acknowledge. Swarms of mosquitos hovered over puddles of putrid water out front, and Violet's vegetable garden wasn't just dead, it was rotten and reeking.

Cory lifted her skirt and hopped on the front steps as she realized Violet was right and it was dozens of scorpions scuttling across the yard that kept the chickens so busy.

The screech of a rusted windmill would not have grabbed Jess's attention beyond its annoyance except that the blades spun one way and then the other.

Augie cocked his head and gave him a look. "Peculiarities."

The house next door to the Gallaghers' appeared to be abandoned and when Cory asked about it, Violet wailed, "No one wants to live next to a haunted house that's next to a cemetery."

The cemetery was not directly along their opposite property line, but it was close enough that Cory could count the crows lined up along its fence.

The hair stood up on their arms as, ignoring it all, Frank led them inside. The flames roared much too high in the fireplace and every burner on the cast iron stove was lit. The grandfather clock near the front window seemed stuck at one o'clock, chiming over and over and over until Mark stuck his hand out to stop the pendulum.

"There's gold in those mountains," Frank repeated, "I found this myself just last month." He held up a nugget that Jess figured to weigh about two grams. "I'm not really a miner, you see, but I *am* a businessman."

"This is no mining town," Jess argued. He hadn't been there long, but he couldn't imagine sleepy Main Street overrun with that kind of crowd.

"We get in before the others, you see," Frank continued, "with places like this boarding house." He swung his arms wide. "We'll advertise a more civilized atmosphere than say, Jerome."

Any place was more civilized than Jerome, Mark thought, but he said, "It's not the place, it's the kind of people it attracts, what gold attracts—"

"Gold attracts more gold," Frank interrupted. He led them to the back of the house where he'd knocked out the wall behind the kitchen and erected wooden frames that would be the bones of the addition. Though a breeze whipped through the opening, the air around them seemed heavy.

"What's this?" Jess wandered over to a large crate stored in what looked to be another proposed room on the other side of the hallway.

"That's to be the bathing room—the fanciest of our amenities!" He lifted the top of the crate to reveal a copper bathtub, still partially covered in shredded shipping material. "I'll also be expanding the dining room and down this hallway will be four guest rooms— two on each side."

As he finished his sentence, all the eggs in a wire basket cracked, oozing yolk onto the table.

Violet only gave the mess a casual glance, confirming everyone's suspicion that such events were normal for her. She stared at the table for a moment and then staggered toward the sofa. It was an exquisite tapestry scroll-end settee that, due to the construction, had been exposed to the elements long enough to veil her in a cloud of dust when she flopped down.

"I sure do miss St. Louis," she mumbled to herself.

Cory's cheeks burned with anger at how easily Frank dismissed his wife's concerns. The poor woman was not hysterical, she was terrified and rightly so. She left the men in the back, turned off the stove and toured the house slowly, running her hands over various items and pausing briefly to pat Violet's shoulder.

She'd received no vision when she walked in, and no spirit had revealed itself, but clearly something was working hard to get the Gallaghers' attention. Other than how the entity manipulated them, there was nothing of significance about the couple's lovely things. The enormous kitchen table, the German grandfather clock, the elegant marble fireplace mantle, and the delicate porcelain dishes revealed little, and Cory found no knickknacks or seemingly sentimental items anywhere in the home. The couple had simply gathered the possessions, purchased with indifference and unloved.

A scent had permeated the rooms, however, since they'd stepped over the threshold. Cory initially labeled it as decay but when she breathed in, she realized it was the smell of…age. The modern and fashionable items in the home didn't fit with the atmosphere of the place at all.

The others took notice of Cory's examination and abandoned Frank's presentation. Undeterred, he moved to stand over his wife, droning on with plans she'd heard a hundred times before until Violet shushed him with a hostile glare.

"This doesn't feel like a haunting. Do you think the place might actually be possessed?" Mark asked Augie

"Only one way to find out." Augie gripped the cross hanging around his neck, then took a tattered bible from his coat pocket and began flipping the pages.

"What if it doesn't believe in your god?" Cory asked him.

"Evil is evil," Augie shrugged, "the condition is treated the same."

She took a deep breath. "This house has a character, not a condition."

Mark smiled at her and turned to the preacher. "What if its older than your god?"

"Then it becomes your problem." Augie snapped the Bible shut.

Mark scanned the room. "It could be a Doler Hob."

"What's a Hob?" Jess wondered.

"There are all kinds, but a Doler will move in and feed on suffering," Mark said, "and it will make things worse if it can, so it doesn't starve to death."

"It didn't have to work that hard, you know," Violet offered, "It could have survived for a hundred years on my misery."

Cory's gaze traveled to the wooden beams across

the ceiling and then the Spanish tile on the floor. She reached out her hands, this time with her eyes closed. Jess put an arm around her waist, gently guiding her away from various obstacles until she knelt and pressed her hands against the dirty floor.

Soon after she jumped up as if her fingers had been burned. Her eyes flew open, wild and afraid. She felt as if the house were shrinking around them, sucking out all the air as it did so.

"Cory?" Jess reached for her, but she ran for the door, stopping outside only when she found herself caught, twisted in the sheets that hung on the line. Panic stricken, she ripped down one sheet and then another and another, further tangling herself in a mass of white cloaks until Jess pulled her into his arms.

His grip was tighter than necessary, and he was afraid that in his earnestness he'd hurt her, but she could not remember when she'd felt so safe and surprised them both by clinging to him with her arms wrapped around his middle and her cheek against his chest.

He rested his chin on the top of her head, and they held each other there, enjoying the closeness despite the bizarre circumstances. It was a feeling they both would have liked to preserve but the foundation of the house had begun to shake, and everyone ran outside behind them.

"What is it, Cory?" Jess whispered in her ear, "Talk to me."

"It's not a demon or a ghost or a...Hob. Whatever it is, it's frightened."

A crashing noise came from out back and Frank's shoulders sagged as the wooden construction frames splintered and fell away from the rest of the house.

Augie said, "I told you that this town has opinions about—"

"We are leaving this place," Violet cut him off, "or I am leaving you, Frank." She ran to her bedroom and began stuffing things into a bag.

The group followed her inside while Frank protested.

"This is our dream, Violet," he insisted.

She straightened her shoulders and the look she gave him shook the other men to their cores. Her eyes were clear, and her voice was calm as she exerted her newfound resolve.

"It is not my dream, and I am done here."

Frank stood on the doorstep, looking back and forth from his wife to the others and then finally at the ruined construction. His ruined plans. It made no sense to him that a house could decide its own future, let alone an entire town. He could not comprehend that the desire to protect the space from outsiders was older than the house, even older than the town. Or, that it ran deeper than any gold nuggets buried nearby.

What he did understand was money and while he would surely lose his investment in the failed hotel, he would lose much more if Violet divorced him. He studied both of them in the full-length mirror, really looked for the first time in ages, and he was astonished by what he saw.

Truly the only ghosts in the house were him and his wife—thin, dull and haggard after months of pointless labor. The bloom had long left poor Violet's hollow cheeks and he was then full of regret. A bit of memory poked into the forefront of his mind—had he not promised her a baby when they first arrived? It would take more than the promise to keep an old promise if he wanted to win back her love. And cost savings or not, he really did want to win her back.

Then Frank's eyes brightened, and he asked Violet if she thought her brother might still want to sell his paint store.

She'd thought her brother an idiot when he opened a store that only sold one product but if Frank was hell bent on losing money, she'd rather it be far, far away from the west.

"Of course you realize," he scratched his head, "that we'd have to move to New York."

Violet's face lit up with a toothy smile and she threw her arms around him. "Let's leave today."

Unlike the others who still held their arms out for balance, the Gallaghers seemed not to notice that the house had suddenly stopped shaking.

Chapter Eighteen

"This doesn't make any sense." Jess pushed a hastily scribbled note from Frank Gallagher across the table for Cory to read. They were back at Marco's restaurant, to redeem themselves for Jess's behavior the last time, but also because Cory wanted more squash.

"It's fried in bacon fat," Doli Salazar confided as she brought out a double portion.

"Just delicious," Cory gobbled down a bite, but her chewing slowed as she read the note and looked up at Jess. "The Gallaghers are giving *us* their house?" She said with her mouth full.

Mark nodded, studying Jess's reaction. "They left all but what would fit in their luggage and they're off to Phoenix in a buckboard to catch a train to New York."

"That's crazy." Cory swallowed hard. "I've never heard of such a thing."

"I've heard a hundred crazy things this week and if I hear one more—"

"Well, now you've got a place to stay while you're in town," Augie cut Jess off before he said something he couldn't take back.

"You expect us to stay in a haunted house?"

Cory shook her head and took another bite. "It's not haunted, remember?"

Jess put down his napkin and leaned across the

table. "Let's not lose sight of what's going to happen here," he reminded Mark. "You're taking us to your mother, who is going to tell us how to defeat Foley and, if we survive, then you're going to help us," he pointed back and forth between himself and Cory, "find my brother. That was the deal."

"But first, you two have to get married," Augie announced.

Cory choked on her squash.

The preacher tried to reason with Jess. "You can't move into that house together if—"

"Are you not listening to me, old man?"

Mark intervened before Jess could get angrier. "If it's alright with you, we'll leave at sunset."

Jess gave him an abrupt nod. "Sunset."

"So," Mark frowned, "If we're going to see my mother, I have to make preparations...for all of us."

"No doubt she'll want to know we're coming," Cory agreed.

Mark sniffed and gave Augie a knowing smirk. "No doubt."

"When was the last time you went to visit her?"

"When I told her that my father died.

Though Mark's expression masked his buried sorrow, Augie's eyes hardened as he remembered in slow motion every detail of the day his best friend was murdered. Seventeen-year-old Mark, on his knees in the dirt with fury in his eyes and his father's head in his lap; and the elder Mark Chisolm's legs still twitching from the violence of the magic that had taken his life.

Oh, young Mark had informed his mother of the tragedy but, of course, she already knew.

"What should we bring?" Cory was anxious that

there was no place in town to buy a bouquet of flowers for their host.

"The less you take with you the better but," Mark looked her up and down and tried to imagine running for his life in that skirt and petticoat, "you should wear your pants."

* * *

Jess wondered if he should whisper a prayer over the message he slid across the counter. It was being sent randomly to the Goodenough silver mine with the hope that Adam would somehow receive it and wait for him in Tombstone. He decided to put his faith in Western Union instead and turned abruptly to leave, nearly running into Mark at the door.

"I had preparations to make as well," he said.

"I'll meet you at the riverbank," Mark told him, "Augie knows the place."

When Jess was gone, Mark held out his hand and the telegraph operator gave him the message, which Mark crumpled before writing one of his own.

"Send this to Clay Hollister," he instructed the operator.

"The Sheriff in Tombstone?"

"The Sheriff in Tombstone."

Mark's insides twisted as he pushed open the door and contemplated the next message he would have to send. It was unlikely to be well received and unlike Jess, he couldn't even trust technology to ensure that it *would* be received since no telegram was ever likely to reach their destination. He chuckled at the thought.

"I wish you wouldn't do that in here," Augie complained.

Mark had made his way to the church. He knelt in the center of a chalk circle with the flame from a black pillar candle the only light in the room.

"What safer place?" Mark stood and stepped out of the circle, then sat down hard on one of the benches with his elbows on his knees.

"Do you think she heard you?"

"Who knows? Maybe this time she'll just kill me and be done with it." He would have been relieved by that notion if such a death weren't sure to be the longest period of suffering known to any man in his generation.

"She didn't kill him herself."

Mark dropped his head into his hands. "She did worse, and now here we are."

"Your father stood up to her. He took you away, gave you a better life, and he trained you to fight—to fight *these* battles." Augie shrugged. "At least you had that. No one even knows what happened to Foley's father."

"He could be imprisoned over there for all we know." Mark shuddered as he spoke. He knew from his mother's prisons.

"Or maybe he's just a god who has no idea what he spawned. What's one more hellion to them?"

"Do you really believe that?"

Augie did not believe it for a second. Any god with the arrogance to think he could trifle with Mark's mother would be in for a shocking surprise.

Mark caught him eyeing Jess and Cory's neatly folded bedding, still separated by the pulpit, and said, "Why don't you just let things happen naturally? Just let them live."

Augie didn't bother to answer him but took the teacher's eraser and went to work on the chalk, glaring up at Mark with a grunt of annoyance at the faint outline of the circle it left behind. "This don't come up. Use salt next time."

Mark smiled to appease his old friend, but he would never risk a break in a salt line, especially when he was calling home.

* * *

After a bit of a panicked search, Jess found Cory in, of all places, the Gallagher house. She wore the pants that Mark suggested, too long and rolled up at the cuffs, a man's tan colored striped shirt with the sleeves pushed up and a bandana around her neck, tied with the knot in front. He moved her long braid aside to reposition the bandana with the knot in back.

"That's better."

"I almost forgot." She dug in her pockets for some hair pins and then twisted the braid into a coil at the nape of her neck before securing her hat.

That getup was about the sweetest thing he'd ever seen, and he almost told her so, but a skittering sound in the kitchen caught their attention. They feared that the house was once again trying to get rid of them, but then a small gray spotted animal with the tiniest ears poked its head out from underneath a tarp.

Jess crouched down for a better look. "That's a kitten—a bobcat kitten!" He exclaimed. "Starving by the looks of it."

He moved to pick it up, but the scrawny thing

backed away, hissing and swiping at his hands. Cory searched the icebox, filled a small bowl and lured it out with what she hoped was not sour milk.

It slurped at the bowl and then sprinted out back. They chased it under the porch of the abandoned house next door where they found another kitten, laying still and barely breathing. Jess searched nervously for the mother while Cory soaked her sleeve in milk for the weaker kitten to drink.

Either hunger got the best of him or the stronger of the two decided that she could be trusted, and he began to slurp at the bowl with enthusiasm while she fed his brother. When the milk was gone, she scooped them up and returned to the Gallagher house where they were then settled into a basket lined with what were probably the most expensive of Violet's cloth napkins.

"We can't keep them," Jess said.

"We're not leaving them here to die."

Jess sighed. His gaze traveled to the open air in the back and the fallen construction. He was shocked that more animals—more dangerous animals—hadn't moved in with the Gallaghers.

Other than the mewing of the kittens, the house was quiet. They moved through the rooms, commenting on the layout and what they would have done differently than Frank.

Cory paused near the copper bathtub. "I have to agree with him on this," she said.

"For you, the bathing room stays," he agreed.

"Except that we're not staying," she turned away from him and pretended to study the fine China in the cabinet. "How can we?"

"Cory, what Augie wants—"

"He's not wrong about how much easier it would be—to travel, I mean."

"What we're doing is so dangerous. Remember that you can leave anytime you want, and I won't try to stop you."

Her head snapped around. "You won't?"

Was that hurt in her voice, or hope? He took a step toward her. "I'd rather you—"

"Mark's waiting at the river," Augie interrupted.

"Christ Augie, why do you have to turn up out of nowhere like that?"

He ignored Jess's complaint and asked Cory, "What have you got there?"

She held out the basket for him to see the kittens.

"Hmm," he gave her a guilty look. "I heard Del Davis bragging that he'd shot a bobcat last night. It was stealing his chickens."

Cory tucked one of the napkins around them as if they might hear and whispered, "Their mother."

Augie nodded. "Afraid so, but we've got to go. Now."

She looked pleadingly at Jess who assured her, "We'll figure something out."

"Are you sure it's a good idea to take her along?" Augie asked Jess.

Jess was not sure it was a good idea at all. Even so, if he were being honest with himself, he knew that he wanted her—needed her—with him, and he hoped she understood that.

"Cory goes everywhere with me, and it's worked out so far."

She caught his meaning, but it rubbed her the wrong way. He wouldn't try to stop her from leaving but that was as close as he would come to asking her to stay.

Mark was already situated in a rowboat when they reached the riverbank. "We cross here," he informed them.

"Hey," Jess shot Augie a look, "you said never cross the river. You said never go to the Other Side."

"To that I hold," Augie said, mainly to Mark, "You've got to be respectful of the borders around here."

"He was right," Mark clarified, "without a guide, you might not make it back."

"Leave that here," Augie held his hand out for Cory's basket, but she clutched it to her chest.

Mark peeked inside and smiled. "This might actually be the perfect gift."

Augie grumbled his disapproval.

Cory had not considered giving Mark's mother the kittens but if he thought she would care for them, then it would be perfect.

Jess heaved another sigh and helped her into the boat, wondering if he would be able to tell the difference between a ghoul and a goblin.

For once, Cory found herself more excited than afraid as they ventured to the Other Side, but the farther Mark rowed away from the shore; the more she worried about meeting his mother. Pleased that she would not be arriving empty handed, she still knew nothing about the woman except that Mark did not appear to hold her in high esteem. At all.

"What is your mother's name?" She asked.

For a while Mark didn't answer and then through

clenched teeth he said, "Her name is Jaya."

In case things went sideways, Augie stayed behind, settling in on the riverbank with his Bible and a burlap sack filled with crystal gems, sugar cubes, candles, sage and salt. Items for practices that some would have deemed to be capital offenses. Since apparently the Good Lord had not anticipated their particular needs, Augie's soul didn't worry too much about having to fight fire with fire when the occasion presented itself. Good Christian soldiers did what they had to do.

Mark had never been a soldier but both mentally and physically he prepared himself for battle as the boat neared the Other Side of the river. Jess and Cory were quiet during the ride, no doubt taking note of the subtle changes in scenery. He began to question the wisdom of bringing them along, but they were a key component of his long-term plans, so it was important that he show them everything, even if he wasn't yet ready to tell them everything.

Cory squeezed Jess's hand to bring his attention to the green glowing scales on the long thin trout skimming just below the surface of the water. But his gaze was focused on the gray potbellied creatures with long ears and longer claws that were crouched between the mesquite trees and he knew at once what they had to be. Goblins.

The trees themselves, while the same variety on this Side as the Other, were fuller and they could tell even in the darkness that the leaves were greener, and their scent was overpowering. Cory struggled to remember if she'd ever even known what they smelled like before.

The water level had risen as they made their way across and it rose again as they came ashore, knee deep waves suddenly splashing around them after they'd disembarked onto the damp bank. When Mark stepped out, as quickly as it had risen, the tide ebbed, and their clothes dried.

Jess and Cory exchanged looks and then she bent to run her fingers through the sand. It almost hurt their eyes, the way the moon light glinted off the grains. What were plain river rocks on their Side were here smooth pink and blue crystals that shimmered under the stars. As she held one up, the ground shifted underneath them, and they grabbed onto one another for balance. Jess took the crystal from her and dropped it back on the ground.

"I'm sure we'll get used to all of this," he muttered to Mark.

Mark's eyes darted in every direction, looking out for trouble. "You'd better hope that you don't."

Chapter Nineteen

Bright and curious eyes blinked out at them from deep caves in the looming canyon walls. Keeping to the shoreline, they followed Mark closely and didn't have to travel but a mile or so before the moon lit up the figure of a woman in the distance. She made no effort to go to them but stood rooted in her spot, impatiently twirling a parasol on her shoulder until they reached her.

Jaya was slightly taller than her son, with brown skin and long black curls that fell in tangles around her shoulders. She'd woven branches from a creosote bush into a circlet atop her head and in the darkness the white fuzzy seed pods almost looked like pearls in a tiara. Her hair was not fashionably styled but her dress had obviously been designed to impress them. Indeed, Cory had sucked in her breath at the sight of it. An off the shoulder evening gown the likes of which that even in her most pampered days she'd only seen in magazines. It was pink velvet trimmed in yellow creosote blossoms draped over silky white brocade with a delicate lace hem that dragged filthy across the ground. She wore no shoes and drew symbols in the sand with her toes as she talked.

"This dress has no train," she said, almost apologetically.

Lovely or not, the dress was utterly inappropriate

for that environment, but Cory was quick to try to console her. "That's very smart. A train would be impractical here."

"You're right of course, but you'll find—or perhaps my son has already told you—" she smiled at Mark, "that I'm not a very practical woman."

"Is that for me?" She snatched the basket from Cory's arms and the bobcat kittens mewed in fear as she whipped the napkins out from underneath them for a better look.

"Oh. How sweet." Sarcasm dripped from her voice, and she eyed Cory with such withering disdain that Cory thought Jaya's emerald eyes might actually burn through her skin.

Jaya stuffed the napkins back in the basket and dropped it in the sand as if it were full of disease. But in the next moment she was like a child, dancing around Mark, hugging him and raining kisses across his cheeks. Mark stood perfectly still through all of this until she grew bored with her own theatrics.

"You came with a request," she clicked her tongue, "so let's have it."

"You know what I want."

"You want to kill your brother," she bopped his nose with her fingertip, "and I want to hear you say it."

Mark wanted to do no such thing, and she knew it. He'd risked coming home to find out if there were another way, even though he feared she would torture him before telling him so.

"If," he said, "if he could be stopped instead..."

Jaya threw back her head and laughed.

"Then tell us what we need to know, woman," he growled, "and I won't bother you anymore."

She narrowed her eyes and positioned herself face to face with him. "Do not treat me with such disrespect."

He opened and closed his fists over and over as he spoke, "You get what you deserve from me after what you did to my father."

"What I did?" Screaming, Jaya marched in a circle around him. "He stole you! That man stole my baby from my arms!" She yanked on her hair, pulling out clumps of curls and unsettling the creosote tiara until it drooped over her left eye.

"He rescued me from your prison," Mark said through his clenched jaw.

Jess and Cory moved to stand on either side of their new friend. Mark did not turn his neck to follow his mother's erratic movements, in fact, his body had gone so rigid that Cory feared he would snap in half if anyone dared to touch him.

Jess peered up into the dark caves and wondered which one young Mark had been kept in and what kind of creature Jaya had engaged to stand guard. He doubted that this woman's choice of nanny would have had a collection of soothing lullabies at her disposal.

As he looked around, an enormous mountain lion leaned over to view the proceedings from her perch atop the ridge, and Jess's heart nearly stopped when he spied her. He worried that Mark would be sucked in as Jaya's grip on reality continued to fade. They could find themselves trapped there without his assistance, such as it was, and the mountain lion would be the least of their worries. Either way, their trip to the Other Side was getting worse by the minute.

"Poor, poor Foley," tears jumped into Jaya's eyes,

"he just couldn't play the game." She favored Jess and Cory with a knowing look as if defending a tantrum throwing toddler rather than a necromancing cannibal. "His powers are not centered around self-control."

Having now met Jaya *and* her 'poor, poor baby', Cory realized Foley could be so reckless with his power that even someone like his mother couldn't deal with it, and she feared him even more than she had before.

Jaya knelt and plucked some crystals from the sand, admiring their shimmer in her palm. "For sure it's a pretty cage," she said, lolling her head from one side to the other, "but we're all trapped here, you know. We're safe as long as we follow the rules, but poor, poor Foley...it is not in his nature to obey."

She dropped the stones and shook Cory by the shoulders, desperate to make her to understand, "*We* have to be patient, *we* have to wait for our moment while our jailer hides silently behind his glorious creation," she shoved Cory away with a sneer, "as if someday we won't fight back." She whirled on Mark and screeched at him, "being part human will do you no favors when we reclaim the world that is rightfully ours."

Mark had heard all of this a thousand times, and he'd even heard rumors that Jaya was half human herself but had *chosen* the Other Side after the flood, allowing it to rot away her sanity over the centuries. He'd long since grown tired of her ramblings and, especially given what she'd done to him and his father, he had little sympathy for her self-inflicted plight.

His voice was low and gravelly as he said, "You owe me this and you know that you do."

Her eyes brightened and her mood lifted considerably. "With my help, you will consider this...debt," she rolled her eyes, "repaid?"

Jaya had no maternal instincts so Mark was reluctant to release her from any other obligation to him but, if he were successful, they would never see each other again and that was worth the risk.

Without further discussion, she held her arms out at her sides and magic crackled around her as she spun in a circle, whispering low at first and then chanting and then screaming until the spirit she summoned finally answered her call.

A twisted mist rose out of the river and hovered there until Jaya's words compelled it forward. It was not willing though and writhed away from her to be closer to the others.

It would have made more of an impact on Mark's friends had the spirit been more cooperative, but Jaya gave up on physical contact with the stubborn ghost and began barking out her commands. The spirit's wail echoed through the canyon, and it flitted from Mark to Cory to Jess as if somehow one of them could save it.

Jaya had specifically selected a spirit who hated her, though Mark figured probably most of them did, as a display of power. All doubt Jess and Cory might have harbored about her abilities dissolved when she forced it into submission.

It was obvious where Foley had gotten his ideas about controlling the dead, but on Jaya's worst day she'd never considered forming an army of ghouls. If she were honest, she would admit to being impressed with her older son's inventiveness. She'd assumed that banishment from the Other Side would end up killing Foley and as always, he'd rebelled with some success but, alas, they had conflicting goals. She was more than willing to sacrifice him, this time to his brother, once and for all ensuring that he would never again interfere with her plans.

She began to pepper the spirit with questions about Foley's whereabouts and when at first it would not comply, Jaya smiled at her visitors and then shouted in a language none of them had ever heard. The spirit emitted shrieks of pain at the sound of her voice and exploded into beads of dew that floated low over the ground until Jaya waved her hands to bring it back together.

As unsettling as it was to see, Mark's mother had made an agreement, and she could turn it into as elaborate a production as she wanted, but she could not break her promise.

Twice more the spirit resisted and judging by its screams, Jaya's punishments were twice as painful.

Cory's stomach turned and she could no longer watch the abuse. "Let it go," she demanded.

Jaya whirled on her. "Do you not call the spirits to you?"

Cory lifted her chin and, thinking of Yvonne and Burl Westin, said, "They seek me out. It is not the same."

"It is exactly the same!" Jaya pulled at the corners of her eyes and stomped up to Cory, "What you do is no different than what I do except that I have significantly more power."

Jess feared that Jaya would make a show of just how much more powerful she was, but instead she cocked her head and waited for Cory's reaction to her insult.

Cory swallowed hard and examined her conscience. It was true that there were plenty of men *and women* who believed her gifts were bestowed on her by the Devil. It was also true that Alain Auclair might have been enjoying his last few breaths because of her revelations to Suzannah. That she thought it good riddance could be considered further proof of her complicity, but she was confident that she'd lost more sleep over his fate than he'd lost over Yvonne's.

Cory had never cultivated her abilities with the intention of doing harm, but she understood that justice without pain is impossible, and Jaya was hell bent on justice, clearly not in the least bit concerned with anyone's well-being. Not her sons' and not even her own, since she must have known that the spirit she tortured would seek revenge.

"I'm no innocent," stepping up to Jaya and lifting her chin in order to meet her eyes, Cory said, "but they will have to burn me alive before I use my insignificant power to be like you."

Jess and Mark both held their breath, but Jaya's demeanor changed again. She laughed and bent to kiss Cory on the cheek. Without looking in his direction, she said, "I doubt Mark is up to the challenge, but what a delightful daughter-in-law you would be."

She returned her attention to the spirit who was by then resigned to submission. "You've been following him for me, now tell me what you see."

"Foley's power is in the beads, infused with a spell." The spirit spoke in soft but raspy tones and all but Cory were surprised that it was the voice of a woman.

Of course Jaya would feel no loyalty to her own kind, but Cory's inner voice reminded her of how close she had come to dismissing the concerns of both Suzannah and Violet and what the ramifications of that would have been.

"Soaked in blood, yes we know," Jaya flopped on the ground, sitting with her legs splayed out in front of her like a child, "now tell us about the spell."

"A wolf's blood heals the wounds you inflicted," the spirit swirled around Mark, "but your brother hunts with more urgency now."

Mark cast a glance at Jess and asked the spirit, "How do we break the spell?"

"He relies on the robust blood of his prey because his blood has so long been depleted of its own vital force. With no energy to power the spell, beads soaked in his own blood will—"

"Kill him!" Jaya raked her hands at her sides and then threw sand in the air. "Easy as pie!"

"Right," Jess said to Mark, and pulled the knife from its sheath on his thigh, "why can't we just cut off the beads and destroy them?"

"His wards are strong," the spirit warned.

Mark agreed, "We couldn't cut through it if Foley stood still and held the necklace out for us."

"Mine!" Jaya moved to all fours and then jumped up, tearing a slit from knee to ankle in the brocade skirt. "That knife is mine!"

"It was your gift to me," Mark argued, "and my gift to him."

"You had no right," Jaya's wild eyes darted back and forth between Mark and Jess, and she screamed, "I want it back!"

The knife vibrated slightly in his hand and Jess looked down to see that the symbols were moving around the hilt as if it was frantically trying to speak to him, but in a language he did not understand.

"You of all people know that a gift is irrevocable—even if I wanted to give it back, you can't have it," Mark said while motioning for Jess to put it away.

Jaya pounded her fists against her thighs and then marched up and down the riverbank muttering one second and screaming the next, pulling at her face and her hair.

The creatures in the caves began to venture out for a better view of the spectacle, including the mountain lion who jumped down from her perch. She circled the basket a few times before poking her nose inside and licking the heads of each startled kitten. After a guarded look around to make sure no one would dare to try and stop her, the mountain lion locked the handle of the basket in her jaws and bounded away into the rock formation above them.

Cory had no time to worry about the fate of the kittens as the spirit slipped next to her. "Leave this place," she whispered, "while you still can."

But it was too late. Jaya stopped in front of Cory and dragged her by the arm toward a thick velvet mesquite that grew near the water. Cory tried to yank herself free, but Jaya's grip was so strong that she feared her arm would soon come away from her shoulder. When she stumbled over the twisted surface roots Jaya shoved her through a mass of low hanging branches into which she disappeared.

Jess sprinted to where she'd been, pushed the branches aside and then circled the tree, but Cory was gone.

It was if a piece of his heart had been cut away and he threw himself against the trunk of the tree, shouting, "What have you done?"

But the trunk wasn't solid, and half of his body was sucked into its softness. Before he could recoil, Jaya checked him with her hip, and then he too vanished.

Mark stomped to the tree, stopping just short of its roots as he knew that not all portals on the Other Side led to the same place every time.

Where did you send them?" He demanded.

She shrugged shoulders, turned and walked away.

He thought about charging after and choking her to death with her precious creosote blossoms. No one would retaliate against him if he managed to kill her, but no one would come to his aid if she tried to kill him, and she most certainly would. Jaya was telling the truth when she said that she was significantly more powerful and not just more powerful than Cory.

So instead, he stood helpless and seething, "I hate you...I hate you...I hate you..."

She never looked back at him, but he heard her call out in a lilty singsong voice, "I know you do."

Chapter Twenty

It took a minute for his eyes to adjust to the light. Soft shades of pink and orange draped the landscape as if Jess had walked into a sunrise. The mountains loomed over him but where he stood was a grove of acacia trees interspersed with the occasional cottonwood. The mesquite he'd come through was nowhere to be found.

Panic tightened his chest but then he turned his gaze toward the sound of rippling water and caught sight of Cory sitting cross-legged in a mound of Mexican feather grass at the edge of a creek lined with yellow wildflowers.

She beckoned to him and with his head spinning, he stumbled like a drunk to reach her, collapsing to his hands and knees and then into her lap. She smiled when he looked up, her eyes so violet in that light that they glowed. His skin tingled as she ran her fingers through his hair and, following an impulse he could not control, he sat up, brought her lips to his, and kissed her long and slow.

"That was nice," she murmured, leaning into him.

Everything was nice. His mind was fuzzy, but he could sense that his thoughts were changing. He stroked Cory's cheek, in the back of his mind recognizing something like a peripheral emotion, a sick feeling of loss that was dissipating more and more with each second.

Cory sensed it too. She could not imagine ever being abandoned, although there was a prickling feeling that may have been the ache of loneliness dissolving out of her memories.

He moved to dip his hand in the clear water, but she took it and kissed his palm. How deep into the Other Side had Jaya sent them? Jess scanned the area but became distracted, picturing the house he would build for her, not haunted, angry or possessed but cozy, near the creek and far away from danger. *Danger.* He pushed the thought out of his mind, closed his eyes and laid back with his fingers laced behind his head.

She snuggled into his chest, and that felt incredible, but passion got the better of him and he rolled her over for a more urgent kiss. Suddenly she knew in her bones that they could have a child on the Other Side, and she arched into him wishing that he would make love to her right there in the grass.

His lips traveled down her neck as he unbuttoned her blouse, but he was interrupted by a harsh nudge at his elbow. He felt more annoyance than fear as he looked up into the eyes of the mountain lion he'd seen on the ridge over the river. The two bobcat kittens leapt around her in the sunbeams, apparently revived and happy in their new home.

She nudged him again with her nose as if to get them up, but why, Jess thought, why were they not allowed the same second chance as the kittens? At first, he and Cory only clung to each other squeezing their eyes closed to shut out the mountain lion as well as the harsh realization that soon came crashing into them both: everything is nice in this place...and everything is wrong.

They scrambled up when the mountain lion bared her teeth, but she circled close to keep them in place until they could see what she needed them to see. They squinted as the cool pink light faded away and the harsh desert sun beat down on them. Their lush meadow slowly eroded into a desolate space. The wildflowers withered and leaves fell away from the trees until they became nothing but blackened stumps. Steam rose from various hollows in the sand where hot springs bubbled just under the surface—indeed the creek where Jess had almost dipped his hand turned out to be a boiling thermal pool surrounded not by delicate grasses but the bones of long dead things.

With their backs together they took it all in and Cory wanted to cry but there was no time. The mountain lion dragged her paw through the dirt in a straight line leading away from the thermal pool.

"Stay on this path?" Jess asked.

She nodded and then used a claw to draw a spoked wheel.

"Look for this?" Cory sputtered, "Is it the way out?"

In the distance they could hear the chittering of a new menace coming their way, and the mountain lion used her powerful shoulder to push them forward along the path she'd provided. They walked single file, one foot in front of the other until the path disappeared. When Jess looked back, the mountain lion was gone but six grayish creatures, about four feet tall with chubby, mottled torsos and long skinny legs ran after them on all fours.

Jess gulped. "Goblins," he said, "go!"

Moving much faster, they forged their own path

keeping as close to the other one as they could manage with the creatures gaining on them. A goblin reached out for Cory but broke through the thin sandy crust before it could grab her.

"Don't look back," Jess hollered over the gurgling screams as it drowned in the boiling sulfur.

The other goblins slowed their pace and gathered themselves in a line behind Jess and Cory.

"They're getting closer," she panted.

Jess pushed her along for another hundred yards or so and then at the sound of a distant rumbling he abruptly halted to take in an enormous formation of boulders off to the side of the path. It was split down the middle as if someone had half-heartedly attempted to create a doorway, and as he peered through the split he could see into an entirely different world.

Behind him were monsters crawling through sand, steam and sulfur but through the stones was a waterfall crashing into a pool surrounded by lush, green grasses similar to where Jaya had sent them via the Mesquite.

Cory grabbed his arm as he moved to step off the path, but he pulled away and said, "It must be over there."

"Jess, please stay with me," she begged, turning him by the shoulders to see the goblins nearly at their heels.

He looked again to the waterfall. *Similar to where Jaya had sent them.* Jess blinked a few times as if waking up from a trance and then a goblin threw a rock that landed in front of the boulders. It popped and sizzled before melting into the sand.

This time they ran as fast as they could and just when their lungs were on the verge of collapse Jess hauled her back by the tail of her shirt and they teetered breathlessly on the edge of a cliff.

The cliff hung over a natural well that had long ago formed in a sinkhole, created by a collapsed cave. He'd heard of such wells used by the ancient ones as their main water source in the otherwise dry landscape. He guessed it was nearly twenty feet below them, but it spanned at least three hundred feet across and if it were not fed by the thermal springs, and if it were deep enough, they could probably survive the jump. *If.*

"There's no steam," she said, "what do you think?"

He looked back as one of the goblins threw another rock. It missed them, plunged over the side and disappeared with a plunk in the black of the well. *Deep enough, no sizzle.* Without saying a word, he just grabbed her hand and jumped.

Coughing and winded from the painful impact, they ducked away from rocks raining down as the screeching goblins reached the edge of the cliff. The water was cool but the surrounding well walls were so slick with algae that they couldn't find a place to climb out.

Cory shrieked as a water scorpion skimmed across the surface level with her nose, but when batting it away she caught sight of a slim rusted metal bar peeking just above the water line on the other side of the well.

"Look!"

They swam toward the metal and away from the falling rocks, which were dwindling in their numbers as the goblins lost interest.

Jess dove under to get a better look and though the water was murky with thick tangles of pond weed woven all through the spokes, the wheel was exactly as drawn by the mountain lion's claw.

"This is it," he panted, but it wouldn't budge when he tried to turn it.

Cory dove under to pull away some of the weeds and came up screaming with a fistful of leeches attached to her fingers.

"Get them off! Get them off!"

Jess had encountered hundreds of leeches in his life, but never so long bodied and never with such long fangs. They'd wound themselves around her wrists and there was a good chance she would drown them both while thrashing around in terror.

He wrapped her legs around his waist and pushed her against the side of the well using one hand to remove the leeches and the rest of his limbs to keep the two of them afloat. Though Cory would disagree, their fangs turned out to be a good thing as he was able to take them by the head and unhook each of them from her skin quite easily. Once destabilized, they unwrapped from her wrists, and he threw them one by one into a floating pile of weeds.

As he removed the last leech, Cory began to hyperventilate. "I can't do this," she gasped, her chin slipping under water after every other syllable, "I can't do it."

A shadow floated overhead, and his own panic level rose at the thought of them trapped in the dark water with creatures likely far worse than fanged leeches after the sun went down.

"I can't either," he assured her, "but *we* can."

He placed her hands on the wheel, pulled Mark's knife from the sheath on his thigh and dove under again. His eyes burned as, horrified, he watched leeches by the dozens float away with the weeds he slashed. Slowly, the wheel began to move under Cory's weight. While she pushed, he braced his feet against the rock wall for leverage and pulled from below but even with the weeds cleared they managed just a quarter turn.

With the sun setting fast they could only afford a few minutes rest before trying again but when Jess went back under, he noticed that the leeches had formed a school and were traveling swiftly toward a lump of something that bobbed in the shallows nearby. His vision was compromised by the murk, but the lump was so large that Jess thought maybe a horse had fallen over the cliff.

It was caught, neck tangled within the pond weeds just above the surface and at the same time being sucked down by a whirlpool of liquified sand bubbling up from the spring that fed the well.

The school of leeches detached from the weeds and raced to attack the trapped beast. It jerked violently to get free, throwing its head back and forth and giving Jess his first clear look at it. He shouted out unintelligibly with excitement when he realized that it wasn't a horse at all. It was Eduardo.

"Eduardo?" Tears sprang into Cory's eyes when Jess told her, and she swam out ahead of him to get to their friend.

"Cory wait, the leeches!" He called after her, but she had already reached Eduardo's slimy cage. He bucked away when she approached but then his eyes widened in shock and relief as he recognized her face.

Jess showed him the knife so he understood the plan and then began to cut away at the weeds while Cory squeamishly unhooked the leeches from his torso.

"How is it possible that you ended up here?" Jess asked him.

"Anything and everything is possible," Eduardo gasped when the weeds came away from his face, "but please, I don't even want to know where *here* is."

"We couldn't tell you if we tried," Cory said.

Once freed from the pond weeds, Eduardo slipped away, pulled under by the whirlpool. His boots were nearly buried in the quicksand but Jess dove down and cut away the uppers giving him enough space to kick out of them.

They led him, still in a daze, back to the wheel where he added his considerable bulk to their efforts. He refused to dip his head underwater but leaned into the wheel behind Cory while Jess pulled from below.

With their combined strength, the wheel turned a complete revolution, and after one more turn, a cavity formed behind it in the well wall. They had only a few seconds to gape at the hole before they, the pond weed, and the leeches were sucked in and swept along a powerful current through a narrow rock tunnel.

The tunnel tapered several feet in, choking off the debris and filtering out everything but the humans who scraped along the sides with the strength of the spring water. Just when Jess felt his lungs would explode, the tunnel shot them out into a much larger body of water and sealed itself up behind them. The current slowed and Jess recognized the trout—the plain old trout that he had fished for the day before. He splashed around until he found Cory and Eduardo, took their hands and kicked up to the surface.

Mark and Augie stood arguing on the riverbank when a wind whipped around them so strong that whitecaps appeared on the water.

"I'm going back for them, but I need supplies and spells..." Mark's voice trailed off as the water bubbled up and Cory emerged with a sharp loud inhale, followed by the two men.

Sputtering and exhausted, they climbed up the bank and collapsed on the sand. Once they'd processed the fact that they were back on their Side, the reality of what had happened hit them hard and took their breath away again.

The Other Side had been full of terrors, but she'd caught a glimpse of a life without conventions and without loneliness, and Cory began to sob like she could never remember doing so before.

After their intense intimacy, Jess was unable to decipher her sadness, which only added to his own. He felt as if all of his potential had been ripped away from him in the tunnel and the crushing sensation of loss that he'd temporarily shed on the Other Side fell back across his shoulders. He rolled onto all fours and heaved, sickened with confusion and frustration and the sense that once again everything and everyone he wanted was just out of his reach.

Only Eduardo seemed unaffected. He flopped on his back and bellowed with laughter, so happy to have been rescued that it would be several days before he would allow himself to dwell fully on the experience.

Cory scrambled away when Mark reached out to comfort her.

"I would have come for you." He tried to sound reassuring, but his voice still carried the angry tinge that

Jaya always brought out in him.

They were too tired to be offended by his tone and too wobbly on their feet to refuse Mark and Augie's help. Jess was particularly slow, walking behind them at a distance and gazing out across the river.

Augie hung back with him and said, "You look like you seen a ghost over there."

His eyes reddened. "The ghost of something that I can't have."

Chapter Twenty-One

For once, Augie was at a loss for words. He'd been stealing glances at Eduardo for an hour and the larger man could take it no more.

"What's the matter old man?" He asked, "Afraid you won't ever be rid of me?"

"You..." he sputtered, "you were dead."

"I was only stuck in the mud." Confused, he mumbled, "I thought you'd be happier to see me."

Augie gave him a grim look. "I thought you'd gone to Heaven."

"Heaven is being home."

"I sure hope not." Augie scratched the back of his head. "I wanted you to be in a better place than this."

Eduardo made a face. He might have gone to Heaven if he'd suffocated in the quicksand, but he might not have, and he would be eternally grateful to Jess and Cory for giving God a little more time to think on that decision.

He took a long deep breath just because he finally could and said, "I didn't get to Heaven, but I'm sure as anything that I caught a glimpse of Hell."

Augie thought he was probably right, and he hoped his friend hadn't gone too far down. He grasped Eduardo's shoulders as if still trying to convince himself that the man standing in front of him was real. Losing friends was all too familiar to him but getting them back was an entirely new experience and he wasn't sure whether to be grateful or suspicious.

At last, he gathered his wits and said, "The next time you're risen up like Lazarus, I'll try to be a little more prepared."

"Jesus didn't raise me, Augie, it was Jess,"

Augie decided against an impromptu sermon on well-placed miracles, and rested a hand over his heart, adding, "Well, the shock of it all nearly did me in."

Eduardo draped an arm over his shoulder and chuckled, "With or without me, old man, I expect that you will live forever."

Augie sighed to himself, "That's what I'm afraid of."

*　*　*

From the steps of the church that evening, Mark heard Augie and Eduardo arguing out back.

Eduardo stood over a wooden crate with his hands on his hips. "You packed up my stuff?"

"I thought you were dead."

"You packed up my stuff."

"Just the things that reminded me of you."

Eduardo knelt and sifted through the crate. True, it was full mostly of his drawings and wood carvings and he began to feel bad about the accusation. Then his lips thinned and he held up the fancy copper coffee pot.

"I *thought* you were dead."

Eduardo snatched up the crate and carried it back inside his little house, grumbling, "Crazy old man."

"I'll come by later," Augie called after him.

He caught sight of Mark walking into the church and headed over to see about defusing a much more dangerous conversation. Jess had just about had his fill of the lot of them, and it was well past time that they gave him the answers he deserved.

"What are you?" Jess growled as Mark pushed through the door.

Mark took notice of the notebook in Jess's lap and the worn-down pencil in his left hand. "Are you documenting your experiences over There?"

Jess had started by trying to puzzle out the trajectory between the quicksand where they'd lost Eduardo in the first place and their location on the Other Side when they found him, but then he remembered that the tree Jaya sent them through disappeared. She probably didn't even know—or care—where they'd gone, and for that he hated her even more. The natural portals were unpredictable, but the mountain lion must have known for sure that the sealed tunnel behind the wheel would lead them back. So, where had they been?

"I'd like to hear about it," Mark said.

Jess grunted. The experience of knowing Mark had left him with a fear of snakes and a fear of water and, he glanced at Cory sleeping near the pulpit, a desperate longing for something he'd never before considered a possibility.

"I don't feel like reliving it for you."

Mark crouched and pulled the blanket over Cory's shoulders, swiveling his head as Jess snapped his book closed. It was time.

"I said what are you?"

Mark sat down hard on the bench. "I am one-half Glaswegian."

"And the other half?"

Mark shrugged, "Goddess, witch, demon? Some combination of all three? I do not know the circumstances that lured my father from Scotland to New York in 1821, but I do know that gold is what lured him out west."

"And Jaya lured him to the Other Side?"

Cory woke to the sound of their deep voices and sat up with her chin on her knees, hanging on every word. Not that she wanted to meet her again, but she'd found Jaya to be as intriguing as she was terrifying—a combination of personality traits that every one of her new friends seemed to possess.

Mark gave his head a mournful shake. "I don't know how long he lived with her over There and neither did he. All I know is that one day he was gone, and she was furious."

Cory gathered from the way he winced that Jaya had taken out her fury on her son and she wondered how old he was at the time.

"He came back with Augie and, like she said, they stole me away."

"You said they saved you."

"It's not that I'm ungrateful," Mark smiled and shrugged again, "but she would have eventually lost interest."

"Lost interest? But then why even—"

"To trap my father? Curiosity? Boredom? Who knows?"

"But you have powers too." Cory interrupted.

"Like you," Mark winked at her, "I can see things

but, unlike you, I can do it whenever I want. I searched for my father in my mind, and I could see him coming back for me. I wasn't afraid but," he grimaced, "I also learned that my mother would become the absolute bane of my existence."

Cory thought for a moment and then felt immense sympathy for him. Her random visions had so far never broken her heart. "You knew your father was going to die."

Mark nodded, "But over Here those powers aren't as strong, the future is fuzzy, so I focus on people instead."

"Using people?" Jess smirked.

"Understanding them."

Jess was unconvinced and said as much, but Mark had been ready for that.

"What good is seeing the future anyway?" He asked Jess, "It didn't stop my mother from trapping you over There."

"How do we," Jess gestured between himself and Cory, "fit into any of this?"

"Coincidentally, Foley chose you for his hunt, and you need my help to defeat him. Independently, I can't see your future, but I *can* see what you need."

"If that were true," Jess argued, "you would have left me alone to find my brother?"

"Not what you want, my friend, what you *need*."

There was a loud rapping at the door and then the livery man peeked sheepishly around as it swung open.

"I'm sorry Miss Lindsay," he said, taking off his hat, "but that wretched mare of yours has run off."

Cory stood up. "Run off?"

"Last I saw, she was headed toward the cemetery."

"You didn't follow her?"

"I'm not..." he stammered and gestured to the outside with his hat, "Well, it's dark now."

Cory grabbed her shawl and pushed past him. "Good lord."

"We left the horses alone for too long," Jess said following her out.

Priscilla was not accustomed to being ignored and she did not approve of Pepper's unflurried nature. From their stalls, they'd seen their humans walking around in town and while that was consolation enough for Pepper, Priscilla required more attention and so she set out to get it, albeit in the wrong direction. She found herself first turning in circles amongst the gravesites and then face to face with a small ghost poised atop a stone inscribed with the words, 'Sandra Sprouse—Daughter'.

Sandra recalled the first time her father lifted her onto the back of a horse, a palomino named...*what was his name?*

Priscilla backed away uneasily when Sandra reached out to touch her. At this rejection, the ghost appeared to disappear in a huff, but when Priscilla looked up, there was the transparent little girl standing on the fence post. She reared up in a panic, kicking over the stone and part of the fence before she heard Cory's voice behind her.

"Were you afraid I'd left you behind?"

Priscilla stubbornly turned her head, but did not move away when Cory ran her fingers through her mane.

"Does this mean we're becoming friends?"

Priscilla was not going to be her friend, but she would rest her head against Cory's shoulder for a minute or two—only until she could relax, of course.

Jess put his elbow on the fence post and then stopped short of letting out a yelp when Sandra's spirit sat down on the railing. She adjusted her pinafore, primly folded her hands in her lap, and blinked at him.

"Are you seeing this?" He whispered to Cory.

She knelt and righted the stone, barely able to make out the inscription in the moonlight, but her heart ached when she did. The cemetery was small, with a marker at nearly every available plot. An eerie haze floated over the graves which were dusty with weeds grown up over most of the stones. Had the little girl's family moved on? How many of these souls had been abandoned? She would ask Chester Wilder about it later.

Having studied the grown-ups for a while, Sandra decided that they presented no threat, hopped down from the fence with a wave, and disappeared in the tall grass.

Jess shook his head thinking that they should have been beside themselves from the experience, but by then he was simply grateful that the tiny ghost wasn't hostile. Cory seemed to agree, returning her attention to Priscilla and nuzzling her neck while the horse feigned indifference.

Jess thought back to the way Cory responded to his kisses on the Other Side. The way she touched him and the soft noise she made when his leg had slipped between hers. It seemed that nothing had been real over There, but on this Side or the Other Cory *had* warmed to him, and she was devoted to his cause, but would that be enough?

Falling in love was never in his plans. A wife and a home had always been so far out of reach that he'd never even let himself dream about such things. But what were the plans anyway? Find Adam and continue life as usual? Aimlessly wandering Arizona with their guns for hire?

Even if a wedding was a only pretense for propriety, he had to admit that his feelings for her, when he allowed himself to have them, were getting stronger every day. If Foley was coming for them, they might only have a few days left and he hated the idea of spending them in doubt.

"I've been thinking about what Augie wants from us," he said, "Do you think we could ever—"

"Seeing as how we're already partners, it *would* make things easier for us," she interrupted, "but don't misunderstand, I'm not just looking for someone to make an honest woman of me, in fact I detest that phrase—"

"Dammit woman, I asked you a question. If you don't want to live with me, just say so."

At that Cory grew silent. Her failures were mounting. She left Chicago to make her own way in the world, on her own terms. Since then, she'd almost been killed three—no four—times in as many weeks. It was not exactly how she'd envisioned her newfound freedom, and she'd certainly never envisioned meeting a man like Jess Carson.

Whether she liked it or not, Jess had stolen her heart, but he didn't know what to do with it and that made her nervous. She'd known her first husband for years before they married but he was distant and cold and even as she walked down the aisle it felt wrong— so wrong.

Though they'd only known each other a short time,

and though he was clumsy with his emotions, she could not stop thinking about how warm it was in his arms and how loving Jess felt so right.

His frustration with her was building but before he gave up in disappointment, he asked one more question. "What are you so afraid of?"

What am I not afraid of? She thought to herself.

"It's not that I don't want to live with you," she answered finally, "it's that I don't think I want to live without you, and that's what I'm afraid of."

His heart jumped into his throat, and he swallowed hard.

"Oh, Jess, what are we doing? I knew it would be dangerous out west, but I expected miners and brothels and bar fights. I did not expect sorcerers, ghosts or other dimensions."

He surveyed the darkness. A cemetery was the last place he ever wanted to be, let alone where he wanted to discuss his future but for the two of them it seemed the perfect place. It was at least the most peaceful place they'd been together yet.

He took her hands, pressed her fingers to his lips and then said, "Marry me, and I promise that we'll figure it out."

They led Priscilla back to the livery stable, visited with Pepper for a while and then knocked on the door to Augie's small house. He wasn't home but as they turned to walk back to the church, the door to Eduardo's house flew open and he called out to them.

Cory poked her head around the big man to get a look inside and found Augie by the fire with a cup of coffee in his hand.

"What fresh hell have you brought with you now?"

He asked them.

"Since it was your idea, you're gonna have to tell me," Jess joked.

Cory made a face at him and said to Augie, "We would like for you to marry us. Before we're murdered by Mark's brother, if possible."

Augie beamed at Eduardo and then back at them. "How about tomorrow?"

Chapter Twenty-Two

He was not particularly fond of the nighttime or the cold, both of which necessitated a fire, but Foley could appreciate that the cover of darkness provided him with unsupervised access to his more questionable resources.

The souls in that cemetery were too long dead to make useful soldiers but their spirits could be put to work. It had been his experience that in life women were, at best, unpredictable and in death they were downright insubordinate. But life in that town had been particularly difficult for child-bearing human females, so their graves far outnumbered those of men. They would have to do.

He had fashioned himself a new club, similar to the brakeman's but with a longer handle and a thicker, heavier head into which he'd hammered four long nails that protruded nearly an inch from each side. Foley held it up to the moonlight, admired it briefly and then set it aside to commence his spell work.

As expected, the spirits were unwilling to comply but, like his mother, he knew how to convince them. He was particularly fond of the black magic practiced by the Indigenous witches, but those witches could only dream of the power he wielded when weaving their spells alongside the knowledge Jaya had passed down to him.

The desperate wailing of the spirits caught the

attention of the little ghost who played with a coyote pup across the yard. A precocious nine-year-old in life, Sandra Sprouse had appointed herself Grave Watcher in death, patrolling the cemetery at night to keep the more restless of her kind inside the gate. It was not often that anyone dared to invade her grounds, and she smiled to herself as the pup followed her to where Foley knelt between two graves.

He ignored the pup until it latched its jaws onto his bag in a ferocious tug of war that emptied most of its contents in the dirt. Swearing, he reached for his club, but the pup easily leapt clear of his swing. The coyote was annoying but small and Foley outright laughed at its growls until he noticed the Grave Watcher standing over them.

Waving her away he continued with a chant that raised two angry spirits out of their resting places. In a tearful rage, they cried out to the Watcher and Sandra lunged for Foley, squeezing her fists around his narrow neck. He pried her fingers off one by one and tossed her away like a rag doll.

Once during her life, a rattlesnake had struck at Sandra and though it missed, she'd been hysterical for hours afterward. Her father explained that the snake was afraid that she would hurt it and since he was raising three daughters in an uncivilized environment, he'd turned the event into a teaching opportunity.

"Whenever someone tries to hurt you, pretend that you're a snake and bite them."

Sandra picked herself up, smoothed her dress and turned her back on Foley, who was satisfied that he'd made his point. As the spirit's cries grew more desperate, her eyes narrowed into slivers and her ears twisted into sharp points.

The crows that had been sleeping in the trees flew down to line up along the fence, watching with great interest as the Grave Watcher transformed.

Her fingernails grew long and sharp, and her mouth widened to nearly half the size of her head in order to accommodate the long fangs that extended down past her jaw.

As before, she leapt at him but this time he was unable to pry her fingernails out of his neck and cried out as she sank her fangs into his cheek. He clutched his necklace and shouted a spell that thrust her backward, but not before she tore away what was left of the skin stretched across his jaw.

He swore again and smoothed his hand over the wound, pulling the skin back to its proper place. "You are a wretched little thing," he sneered and lunged for her, but did not expect the crows to flock to her aid.

They circled his head and dove at him one at a time, their sharp beaks puncturing holes in his skull. His hand blindly scratched at the dirt, searching for the club until at last, he rose up, swinging wildly and scattering the birds far enough away that he could escape. Once outside the gate, they did not chase him. He spit in their general direction, but the attacks were of no consequence.

Foley had expected nothing but oddities after realizing that Carson had led him back to Mark's adopted hometown. The injury sustained from the Grave Watcher was unpleasant but his work in the cemetery was complete. Nothing but the final battle of the hunt would keep him from breaking the curse and living a life in which hunts were merely desired rather than required. Practically able to taste his freedom, he grabbed his club and his bag and ran toward the gate.

Returning to her sweetest form, Sandra picked up the supplies that had fallen from Foley's bag and, because she didn't wish to banish the spirits, flung the salt over the fence. Her mother had been a healer and though she could not cure the infectious fever that killed her daughter, she'd given Sandra plenty of instruction.

It served him no purpose, so Foley had paid no attention to the purple sage growing wild along the borders of the cemetery; but Sandra gathered as much as she could hold and sprinkled it over the graves of the ones he'd tried to bind to him. Then she did the same with Foley's supply of valerian, known to induce bad dreams but also known to undo the workings of witches.

The spirits were doubtful but, as the sun rose, the Grave Watcher set her spell and skipped away with the coyote pup on her heels and with the hope of another visit from the horse and her lady.

* * *

Drizzly and dark, it was a dismal day for a wedding. Cory stared out the window of the Gallagher house wishing that her sister Julia was there with her but let out a grateful sigh as she caught sight of Doli Salazar stepping lightly up the front steps.

"Is it so awful?" Doli reached out and took her hand.

The question took Cory aback. "Awful?"

"It's bad luck to look so sad on your wedding day."

Doli's grip tightened. "Are you afraid of him?"

Cory rolled her eyes. "Afraid *for* him, more like."

Doli considered what she knew about Jess. "That's fair." She loosened her hold a bit, but her internal alarm was still raised. "If he beats you, I'll call for Marco right now—"

"He certainly does not." Cory paced the room, "I realize that he's got a lot on his mind, what with being hunted by a mad sorcerer and all, but I don't know what he really wants from me."

Doli blinked at her. "What difference does it make what he wants?

Doli hadn't married Marco for love. They were both widowed and met later in life via an unfortunate real estate dispute between their families. Their union had been a practical arrangement that financially benefited everyone involved, and their friendly marriage suited them. He treated her kindly and, in accordance with their contract, made her half owner of the restaurant. They worked well together and over the years had settled into a comfortable existence, but Cory had a strong feeling that Doli missed her first husband terribly.

In Cory's case, there was no comparing her ex-husband's cold, hasty touch to Jess's hungry kisses, but she feared all that passion might have been relegated to the Other Side.

"It's just that his feelings are so on and off that I can't decipher them most of the time."

"Psh!" Doli scoffed, "men can't decipher their own feelings. And honestly, would you ever really want them to? What a mess that would be!" She thought for a moment and asked, "Will he keep his promise to you?"

Cory said, "I believe that he will." And she did truly believe that.

"Then worry about what you want for now."

She looked Cory up and down fearing the frayed hem on her skirt mirrored the woman's nerves. "Is that what you're wearing?"

Cory led her to one of the bedrooms and threw open an enormous wardrobe.

"Violet left me everything in here. I was hoping something more suitable of hers would fit, but I can't decide."

Doli also thought it bad luck to wear someone else's clothes, but at least Violet wasn't dead—as far as they knew.

She pulled out a crisp white cotton nightgown and held it up to Cory. The garment had a button closure from the neckline to the waist and was trimmed with pink lace at the sleeves and the hem. She tossed the matching dressing gown on the bed.

"Have you thought about tonight?"

Cory turned away, smoothing the lace on the dressing gown. "It's not something I looked forward to when I was married before." *To say the least.*

Doli was sympathetic but, as always, ready with advice. "My sister-in-law keeps a flask in her dresser drawer for those occasions."

"Good lord."

"Every man is different, so you never know."

Cory's stomach flipped. *You never know.*

"I suggest getting lost in those big brown eyes of his."

So, Doli had noticed that too. "I've been trying to avoid them."

"Well honey, now's not the time for that."

"Save some for later," Eduardo grumbled, swatting Augie's hand away from the cake. At Eduardo's request, Eileen Daggett had been happy to bake a little cake for Jess and Cory, knowing that she would be reporting any juicy gossip about the mysterious couple as early as that afternoon. To be sure that everyone in town also heard about her excellent baking skills, she decided on a vanilla round cake topped with honey-soaked orange slices that made Augie's mouth water.

The cake sat protected from the elements atop a small wooden table shaded by a sycamore tree on the riverbank where Jess, Augie, Eduardo and Mark milled about uncomfortably. Through word of mouth, Augie had invited the whole town, but the curious crowd in attendance was small: Chester Wilder with notebook in hand, Asa and Eileen Daggett, and Marco Salazar.

To everyone's relief, the clouds parted slightly and there was only the light patter of scattered rain drops on the water.

Mark pulled two golden bands from his pocket and handed them to Jess.

"I can't afford these," Jess whispered to him.

Mark waved him off. "There's plenty of gold in those mountains," he said, glancing across the river.

"I thought everyone who went looking for it died."

Mark shrugged. "I didn't go looking for it."

Before he could get those interesting details, Mark waved him off again and they were interrupted by the approaching wheels of the Salazar buckboard.

Cory eased herself down from the wagon and

smoothed out her dress. It was not really *her* dress that she was wearing, but she could hardly believe it was *her* life that she was living. Both were a little big on her, but both had a lot of promise.

The dress she'd selected was a matching cream-colored skirt and blouse dotted with lemon yellow flowers. It had a scoop neckline that bared more skin than she ever had before, and her hair fell in long curls over her shoulders. She wore it long but neatly pulled back with a matching yellow silk bandeau.

Doli noticed Jess's wide-eyed expression when he caught sight of Cory, and she gave her a look. "I doubt you'll be needing a flask."

Jess sucked in his breath. He'd filled his notebook with descriptive language about the elegant saloons he'd stopped in, the whispering pines he'd ridden underneath, the vile coffee he'd choked down and the frigid lakes he'd fished in, but he had a hard time describing Cory. She was just so damned pretty, and that was all he could ever come up with.

Eduardo ran out to greet them and gave Cory his arm, walking slowly to keep her steady on her feet. Everyone there knew that the circumstances surrounding the wedding were not ideal, but Eduardo was certain that, assuming they lived out the week, she and Jess would be happy together.

Cory could not help returning his warm smile, recalling how her stepfather had practically raced her down the aisle, so delighted was he to be relieved of the burden of her existence.

As Eduardo escorted her to an already anxious Jess, everyone's heads snapped around at the sound of René's horse splashing through the mud. Having ridden all night, he was breathless and nearly leapt from his saddle, staring right at Cory while everyone in the small crowd stared at him.

"My apologies," he said only to her, "for being late."

Jess narrowed his eyes. "You were invited?"

Eileen gasped and whispered loudly to her husband, "Do you think they'll have fist-a-cuffs over her?"

"Shush," Doli scolded.

Eileen could not believe her luck and only grew more excited. "Will Mr. Carson shoot him?"

Doli snarled in her direction and Eileen crossed her arms in a pouting fit but inched closer to listen intently.

"It's nice to see you again," Cory said, but even though she could feel René's eyes burning into her, she turned her attention back to Jess and gave his arm a squeeze.

Mark gestured for Augie to start the ceremony and led René out of earshot to the other side of the tree.

"She deserves better," René grumbled under his breath.

"Of course she does," Mark agreed, "but you're not the one."

"You know her heart?"

Mark shook his head. "I know his."

More accustomed to conducting funerals, Augie fumbled the words a bit, but the gist of the ceremony was clear, and everyone kept a side eye on René when the preacher asked if anyone could show just cause why the couple should not lawfully be joined together in matrimony. René stiffened when invited to speak now or forever hold his peace, but Mark gripped his shoulder and held him still.

"Let them have this," he said.

René pounded the tree trunk with his fist and glared at Mark as the newly pronounced man and wife shared a kiss.

His pride was wounded for sure and for the first time in a long time, his heart truly ached. From the moment she entered Alain's parlor, René had known that Cory Lindsay was special. He would have to bear his loss while also bearing witness as Jess Carson blundered through his good fortune. Even so, it was time to focus on the other reason he'd raced into town.

René scanned the mountains and the river for some sign of the trouble to come and then plucked a honey coated orange slice from the cake, tipping his head back to drop it in his mouth. Then, before sauntering away from the festivities, said to Mark, "Foley is here."

Chapter Twenty-Three

Cory carried what was left of the orange cake as they walked home to the Gallagher house. It was delicious and though she knew that Eileen Daggett was even now engrossed in a dramatic recital of the events of her thankfully non-dramatic wedding, there was no denying that the woman was a culinary genius.

Jess had declined his piece, which Augie cheerfully snatched away.

"More for us," Eduardo joked, "besides, you have the look of a man who could use some roughage instead."

What Jess could have used was more time but, according to Mark, Foley was close. So, while scanning the road for danger, he put his hand on Cory's back to nudge her along.

"Officially home," she announced, placing the cake on the kitchen table.

"For now," Jess mumbled, glaring into the breeze coming through the construction gaps. He gathered up a tarp and set about covering it up.

"Mark said Foley is hiding out somewhere here in town, so you should get some rest while you can."

She looked from the bedroom back to him and blinked. "Rest?"

"Rest." He searched around until he found a

hammer and turned back just in time to see her slam the bedroom door behind her.

With minimal injury but much swearing under his breath, the tarp was secured. He tossed away the hammer, ruminating over the fact that while it would be less breezy, he hadn't really made them any safer and that his new wife had gone to her room with tears in her eyes. *His wife.*

He closed the window in the second bedroom, hung his gun belt on the bedpost and then sprawled on the chair. Again, he thought, *Adam would never believe this.* He'd always followed up that thought by wondering how Adam might advise him, but Adam wasn't there, and he might never be there again. The reality was that Jess was no longer just the little brother. He had his own tiny family now and his own big problems and it was time to start thinking about what *he* would do.

The walls in his room contracted with a groan and the picture hanging over the chair slipped from its nail, cracking the back of his head on its way to the floor.

"God dammit." Rubbing his head, he picked it up and gaped with recognition. It was a drawing signed by Violet Gallagher of the exact spot near the river where he'd been married only a few hours earlier; probably drawn when they first arrived in town. She'd sketched an owl perched in the sycamore tree. He'd always been taught that owls were bad luck, but he was just then determined to disprove that legend.

Jess figured that Cory thought she'd been saddled with another mean husband, and he couldn't bear her imagining him that way. He would not have them sitting alone in separate rooms on their wedding night when at the very least they could sit together and plan their future, nontraditional as it was bound to be. He decided to bring her another piece of cake and start the conversation.

Every one of them impractical to the point of ridiculous, Cory sorted through the dresses in the armoire while over and over her mind replayed her wedding day kiss. Jess had pulled her to him with an intensity that surprised the two of them as much as it did Eileen Daggett. Yet, he'd just sent her away like a child who needed a nap.

She leaned in close to the mirror and ran a hand along her face, scowling at some tiny new lines around her eyes before stripping off her dress and wriggling out of her underclothes. She examined her entire naked body, twisting to get a look at every curve and every scar, finally touching the inflamed stitches in her side. They would have to come out soon.

The nightgown Doli left on the bed was lovely and it fit just fine and maybe someday her husband would see it on her. *Maybe.* Unable to hold it back any longer, her face scrunched up and she threw herself across the bed to sob quietly into the pillows.

But Cory was tired of crying. She pounded her fist against the mattress and pushed herself up. Before losing her nerve, she made a final sniffle in the mirror, fluffed her hair around her shoulders and threw open the door to find Jess standing there staring at the ceiling with a plate of cake in his hand.

"I thought you didn't like cake," she said, following his line of sight to see what held his attention so rapt.

From the kitchen, Jess had thought he heard

something on the roof, and it seemed to follow him to her room, but whatever it was stopped as soon as she opened the door.

"I thought you might want—" Doing a double take from her to the ceiling Jess took a sharp inhale. The flame from the oil lamp on the dresser backlit Cory's curves through the thin fabric of the nightgown and he ached to hold her. The dim light also highlighted the fact that she'd been crying.

He touched her cheek with his free hand and said, "I know that I'm doing everything wrong."

She took the plate to the kitchen and when she returned, wrapped her arms around him from behind, resting her cheek against his back. He knew that her touch was the closest he would ever get to heaven but instead of taking her into his arms he stood fixed in his spot.

The rustling on the roof had started again and, damn, he wished he was imagining it, but he was sure that he wasn't, and even more sure that awful things were about to happen.

He turned to face her and when she started to speak, he put one finger to her lips and pointed up with his other hand. There was no sound, but a small piece of ceiling dropped between them. Her face fell in disappointment, but she nodded with understanding, stood on her tiptoes and stunned him with a deep heavy kiss. His response to her was immediate and intense but short lived as just then Foley's nail studded club sliced through the tarp behind them and the ceiling caved in from the weight of two ghouls.

Foley pulled back the tarp and emerged wearing a wide grin. Jess instinctively felt for his gun and then dashed for the bedroom where he'd left it, but just as he grabbed it out of the gun belt the two ghouls tackled him onto his back.

"By now you should know that bullets won't work for you," Foley laughed, "but building up your wild energy is what works for me." He grabbed Cory by the throat and pushed her against the wall. "This ought to do it."

Foley was right about that, and Jess roared with rage as he fought to get away from the ghouls. The first one had him straddled while the second dragged the blade of a knife across his hip. They'd been warned not to kill him, so the knife pressure was light, but not so light that it didn't tear open his pants and the top layer of his skin.

Operating under the assumption that he was no longer an uninvited guest, René kicked in the front door, distracting the first ghoul long enough for Jess to shrimp out from underneath its weight.

René threw his knife at the second ghoul, who flew backward over the sofa from the force of the impact to his chest.

Jess blinked at him. "How—"

"Go to her!" René shouted while lunging to keep the first ghoul from taking Jess down again.

Her kicking and struggling only caused Foley to tighten his grip around Cory's neck so she focused on his beads which glowed more brightly than she'd ever seen, the turquoise practically throbbing with power. She took it in her fist and yanked as hard as she could, but the necklace held fast around his leathery neck. She was beginning to see spots from lack of oxygen and changed tactics, reaching around to jerk the strand from behind in hopes of choking him with his own magic.

From the corner of his eye, Foley caught sight of Jess charging toward him, so he slammed Cory's body against the wall and tossed her away. She landed in a daze and when she tried to stand, found her legs tangled up in the long nightgown. After twisting ungracefully on the floor to follow the sound of the screams that echoed around the room, she saw that René had relieved one of the ghouls of an arm, but the other one was biting down on his neck.

As her wits returned, she tore away the hem of the nightgown below her knees and then sprinted to René, picking up Jess's gun along the way. She cocked the hammer and with both hands wrapped around the grip, fired into the torso of the ghoul at René's neck.

Delighted that she'd hit the ghoul and not him, René reconsidered his previous opinion that a woman like Cory should never learn to use a gun.

"You have excellent aim, chére," he said, making sure to hack off the ghoul's head before it could be reanimated.

She moved to tear more from her gown to dress his wound, but he batted her hands away.

"You could bleed to death," she argued.

René thought that he might already be teetering on the verge of just that, but he shook out a handkerchief from his pocket to press against his neck and said, "Let me assure you that exposure to one more inch of your lovely stems would kill me faster than anything else."

She gaped at her legs that, as far as she could remember, had never been exposed in public but before she could respond, the first ghoul whistled out and an enormous half-starved wolf came stalking through the front door. Foley had only needed blood from the first half of the bonded pair of wolves in order to heal himself, but he'd placed her widower under his control for just such a situation.

Jaws snapping and starving, it moved slowly through the room, backing Cory into the ghoul.

"Easy now..." René raised his hands, inching closer and closer but when he was almost between her and the wolf, the ghoul pulled her down by the hair and it was on them before she hit the floor.

Just before René dove into the pile, Cory jumped up, holding the ghoul's severed arm.

"Here boy," she said making her way to the door, "come and get it."

Its mouth watering, the wolf stalked her across the room to where she tossed the arm outside and slammed the door behind it.

René's strength was waning, but he fell on the incredulous ghoul, shoving his knife so far into its throat that the blade wedged into the wood floor underneath them.

René was able to push himself up to sitting, but he could not make it to his feet. Instead, when Cory stood over him, he used his fingers to wipe away the blood that dripped down her leg.

So far, she'd escaped their ordeal with little more than scratches, but he had not been so lucky. She knelt beside him and pressed the handkerchief back against his neck.

"You've done all you can do."

"No, chére..."

"René, please stay here..." she looked around for Jess, "I cannot be worried about you."

He closed his eyes in resignation and said, "Go."

As soon as Foley had thrown Cory away, Jess rushed him with the knife, slashing through the sinews of his arm. Foley lost his grip on his club, but Jess's attack only drew a trickle of blood. Foley's body was made up of little more than ropes and cartilage, so it was going to be difficult to get enough of his blood to break the spell.

Not wishing to reintroduce the wolf to the fight, Mark arrived through the shredded construction entrance and was now at Jess's side.

"This will not go the way you want it to," Foley snarled at his brother, scooped up his club and advanced on the two men.

"It never has," Mark nodded at Jess who dove for Foley's ankles and took him to the floor.

Mark lunged at him, but Foley was fast and flipped over, swinging the club into his back. Mark let out a scream and with a sickening squelch, pulled himself away from the nail. He grabbed Foley's forearm and shoved the club back at him, forcing a nail deep into his forehead.

Howling with fury, Foley pulled the club away and though Mark had buried that nail in his skull, Jess despaired. *Still no blood.*

Chapter Twenty-Four

Cory searched frantically but for the time being, Jess's gun was lost.

"Chére..." René could barely get his voice above a whisper, but he was pointing to the fireplace where another oil lamp sat unlit on the mantel.

She took it down, pulled off the chimney and hurled it at Foley's back. The delicate glass shattered against his frame and soaked him in kerosene.

Suddenly overcome by the memories of his exile and the shock of his mother's treachery, Foley began to panic. The smell of the oil permeated the room, and it would only take one spark...

He backed away from them, gripped the beads around his neck and began shouting the words that would summon the ghosts from the cemetery to his aid.

The spirits he'd worked the spell over did come, but they glided past Foley to surround Cory, pushing her against the wall and dissolving behind her. When she tried to move their misty limbs reached through and held her still.

Foley shouted out the spell once more, but it was the little Grave Watcher who answered his call.

"Sandra?" Jess knelt to meet her at eye level.

Mark was impressed. "You know her?"

"We met at the cemetery." Jess took her opaque

little hands in his. "It's not safe for you here, sweetheart."

Mark pulled him up. "The Grave Watcher is a guardian of the dead and she would never let him exploit those spirits. This is her job." He cast a glance in Foley's direction. "A wiser sorcerer would have remembered that this town takes care of its own."

Sandra gave Jess a little curtsey, then wandered over to the fireplace and struck a match. Foley's face twisted in horror, and they all stepped back as she smiled sweetly and flicked the match at his feet.

Foley tried to stomp out the flames, but the match caught the kerosene on his boots and in seconds they were traveling up his legs. He screamed and sprang at Jess, holding him in a bear hug as they fell through the tarp, engulfed by the fire.

Jess rolled away once they hit the ground outside and slapped away the fire on his sleeves and then felt frantically for the knife. He punched his fist in the dirt, swearing loudly as he realized he'd lost it in the tumble.

Foley landed in a dry hopseed bush that closed around him as it ignited, wrapping his body in the blaze. The fire spread quickly through the neglected brush surrounding the abandoned house next door until it reached the rotted front porch.

Mark had instructed Augie and Eduardo to stay behind the house waiting for his signal in case they needed help. It wasn't exactly what they'd expected but the fact that everything was on fire surely counted as a signal. Augie ran for the town fire fighters and Eduardo for the rain barrel at the side of the house.

Inside, Cory negotiated her release from the spirits by convincing the Grave Watcher that Mark would protect her while she helped Jess, and by promising that she would regularly bring Priscilla to visit the cemetery. Mark raised an eyebrow at that but if Priscilla was to be in Cory's care there were some harsh truths the horse would have to learn to accept.

Without breaking stride, Cory snatched Jess's knife from the floor. Mark could barely keep up with her as she sprinted away, but outside they stopped short, met by a chest high inferno made up of the brittle bushes. Frantically craning their necks this way and that, they searched the darkness with no sign of Jess or Foley. From across town, the hand pump engine rang out its impending arrival, but there was no time to wait.

"Absolutely not," Mark took her arm as Cory prepared to jump through the fiery hedges and was taken aback by the otherworldly way that the violet flecks in her eyes accentuated her anger as she jerked away from him.

Her long curls, littered with dust and leaves, fell wild around her shoulders and the tattered nightgown she wore exposed the many scrapes and bruises across her bare limbs. Clutching the hilt of Jess's knife, she had the look of an ancient peasant warrior and had he not known better, Mark would have thought he'd stumbled onto the Other Side where such a sight would not have been so strange.

As it was, the stubborn Mrs. Carson had made a deal with the dead ones and was in Mark's charge whether she liked it or not, so he grabbed her arm again and insisted, "We'll go around."

She struggled against him, but their argument was short lived as Eduardo cleared their path with water from the rain barrel.

"Give it to me!" Jess stumbled out of the shadows reaching for his weapon.

Foley had risen to all fours, crawling away from the chaos until Cory flipped the hilt around and handed Jess the knife. He plunged it into the back of Foley's thigh, opening up at least a three-inch gash that went all the way through his leg. The protective wards guarding Foley's necklace weakened as blood spurted from his femoral artery and seeped into the dirt. The glowing turquoise beads began to dim, and the connective cord of woven mesquite dried and crumbled away from his neck.

Cory hit her knees, gathering up the beads and stuffing them into Foley's wound. The Grave Watcher, the ghosts and even the crows lined up along the roof and in the branches of the smoldering trees, observing with approval as the new mistress of what was to be The Carson House went to work on her enemy.

Under the weight of Mark and Jess, Foley twisted in agony, using the last of his breath to curse them one at a time, and then he fixated on Cory, for once getting a good look at her determined face. He'd underestimated them all but, in his arrogance, he'd considered her and her minimal power to be little more than a mild amusement. Really nothing other than a detail in one man's life, significant only to Jess. But she was a full force of nature in her own right and it occurred to him then that she would make the perfect host.

Still convinced that Jess Carson's would be the blood that would break Jaya's curse, Foley laughed to himself at the notion of the bounty hunter finding himself hunted by the woman he loved.

Nearly mad from the pain, but running out of time,

he forced his arms to reach for the mirror he kept in his vest. To succeed, every step would have to be focused, which was unlikely, but Foley had nothing to lose as his life dissolved alongside the spell he'd so carefully devised to preserve it.

Jess lifted Cory up between him and Mark, and the three of them stood watching as Foley tried once more to come to all fours. Though he'd concocted a new plan, one that could end with a more satisfying result than he ever imagined, he turned to gape at them, still in disbelief at how spectacularly his hunt had failed.

He was similarly surprised when his jaw fell into the burning shrubbery followed by what remained of his head, twisting away from the flimsy tendons of his neck that collapsed from the weight of it. What was left of Foley's skin charred into flakes, his limbs crumbled underneath him, and his body tipped forward in a ghastly pyramid of smoldering gristle and bone.

Not all dead things can rise. Even an experienced necromancer will, on occasion, encounter a soul that was so intent on crossing over that no spell ever spoken would bring it back from eternal rest. And some souls were immediately swept away, Augie would say to Heaven or Hell, but Foley had arranged for a more flexible afterlife and was not bound for either destination. His spirit was focused. And furious.

Mark gestured to the others as a thin gray mist, quite distinguishable from the smoke, rose out of Foley's body.

"His ghost will haunt this place forever," Cory worried.

The mist drifted over the mirror for a moment and then settled into the glass, oozing under the edges of the ornate metal casing.

Cory picked it up and ran her fingers across the back of it, murmuring, "Such a beautiful thing to be owned by something so ugly."

As she held the mirror to her face, tendrils of Foley's spirit reached out, moving through her hair and caressing her face.

Jess panicked anew. "Mark! What in the hell is happening to her?"

"Cory don't look at it!" Mark shouted and tried to snatch the mirror out of her hands.

She held it away in bewilderment as Foley's ghostly hands moved her face back to the glass.

"Cory!" Jess took her by the shoulders. "Look at me!"

She did look at him, but could not help turning to the mirror, at first alarmed by her haggard appearance and then by Foley's countenance settling over the image of her own. She found herself unable to resist the sensational pull of Foley's desire to consume her and his full hatred of Jess.

She took a step back, tears brimming her eyes. "I don't want to hurt you, Jess."

"He's in the mirror," Mark warned, "get it away from her."

Thicker spirals of Foley's essence reached out from the glass, wrapping around her waist to bind her to him as he seeped inside her body.

The totality of Foley's intention became clear, and her skin crawled with the realization of how he would use her body. But once again, he'd underestimated her.

In a strange and difficult fashion, since coming out west she was living her dream. She looked at her companions and wondered how short-lived it would be. Terribly so, she assumed, and she would allow no one—not even them—to take it from her. Certainly not the ghost of a monster she'd just killed.

Foley's grip tightened as he sensed her resistance and his determination to inhabit her body turned her stomach. She fell to her knees next to a large rock and with what remained of her strength, raised the mirror overhead.

"You can do it," Jess whispered.

She let her hands fall, slamming the mirror down, the shattering of the glass drowned out by the last angry howls of the sorcerer.

With her hands over her ears, Cory started screaming, "Make it stop!" so Mark kicked his brother's remains over the shards and laid a burning branch across what remained of his body, which then went up like a pile of dead leaves.

Chapter Twenty-Five

Mark secured the area where Foley died by sprinkling a poultice of cactus thorns, gun powder and coffee grounds over the sight. They stood around it in a circle, sipping coffee as the ingredients sizzled into the dirt.

"I should plant some flowers to hide this," Cory said.

"That's unholy ground." Augie shook his head. "Nothing will ever grow there again."

Cory made a face. "And our neighbors will always hate us."

"We won't be here for long," Jess said.

Mark dragged his boot through the dirt. "How are your funds?"

They were dwindling, but Jess would never admit it. He wanted to be on his way. He wanted to find Adam.

"Stop right there," Jess warned him, "you said you would help me, not trap me here."

"Why not make a salary while you're looking for your brother?"

"You're not one of those Pinkertons are you? I already told them no."

Mark shook his head. "Not a Pinkerton."

"And I'm not fighting Indians."

"What Jaya told you was true," Mark said, "about the creatures on the Other Side who want to break free." He looked Jess in the eyes. "Some of them already have."

"You want me to kill these creatures for you?"

"Nope. I want you to investigate them. Learn what you can and write it down in your book. We keep a record."

"Who is we?"

"Everyone here, and a few other associates."

"For the government?"

"Hell no," Mark said, "for the people."

"The people have their own lives to live," Jess argued, thinking again of his desire to find Adam.

"Lives lived full of belief in creatures, signs and symbols. People accept the power of vampires, sage and juniper as much as they do the power of God. Maybe more."

Augie made a face at that but said, "Look, you've got a house and you could stay here making it your base between jobs."

Jess's lips thinned, "This house?"

Cory put her hands on her hips and peered through the windows, on the lookout for unusual activity. "I guess it doesn't matter where we go or what we do," she reminded him, "because according to the preacher we're already damned."

"This haunted house would make a mighty nice refuge for the damned don't you think?" Eduardo tapped the siding and then bent to pick up the section that fell off when he did so.

Mark could see that Jess was wavering in his resolve. "If you don't want to do research with me, what *will* you do for work?"

"I could run for sheriff, here."

"Of the town you nearly burned to the ground?"

Jess had to admit that the town would sooner get along with no sheriff before they elected him. They'd already been doing so just fine.

"Why me? Why us?"

Mark thought back to the time he followed Jess and Adam out of Tucson after they'd fought the vampire who murdered Jess's grandfather. Jess didn't understand what he'd seen Walter Sallow do, but from an early age he'd been exposed to the unexplained.

"The two of you have seen things that cannot possibly exist, and you know things that cannot possibly be true. Still, you accept them and respect their power, their...possibility." He gestured to the house which he suspected Cory was beginning to love, in spite of its oddities and Jess's objections.

"The next thing I do is find my brother," Jess insisted.

"Absolutely," Mark promised.

After giving the surrounding mountains another quick survey, Cory worried about their proximity to the Other Side. But frightening or not, she had to admit that it was a beautiful place and that it strangely felt like home. "What did you say the name of this town is?"

Augie held his arms out wide. "You are standing dead center in the town of Chuparosa."

"Chuparosa?" Cory fluffed out her skirt and smiled up at Jess, giving his hand that reassuring squeeze he'd come to rely on. "Well," she said, "I suppose it's as good a place as any."

About the Author

Vanessa Haney grew up in rural Arizona with, tragically, no access to the Other Side. Had there been a portal, she would have gone through it a long time ago. Instead, she makes a happy life in less rural Arizona with her son Connor, her partner Mike, and three cats named Felix, Dusty and Daisy. There she writes, hikes, and watches way too many horror movies.

Sign up to follow her adventures at:
http://www.vanessahaneywrites.com